POVERTY
IN
AMERICA

ALSO BY MILTON MELTZER

AIN'T GONNA STUDY WAR NO MORE
THE TERRORISTS
THE HUMAN RIGHTS BOOK
THE BLACK AMERICANS: A HISTORY IN THEIR OWN WORDS
THE JEWISH AMERICANS: A HISTORY IN THEIR OWN WORDS
THE HISPANIC AMERICANS
THE CHINESE AMERICANS
ALL TIMES, ALL PEOPLES: A WORLD HISTORY OF SLAVERY
NEVER TO FORGET: THE JEWS OF THE HOLOCAUST
MARK TWAIN: A WRITER'S LIFE
LANGSTON HUGHES: A BIOGRAPHY
DOROTHEA LANGE: LIFE THROUGH THE CAMERA

POVERTY
IN
AMERICA

MILTON MELTZER

WILLIAM MORROW & CO., INC.
New York

PICTURE CREDITS

AFL-CIO, 86; AP/Wide World Photos, 49, 60, 74, 100; Kim Hopper, 2, 23; Gray Panthers, 55; Milton Rogovin, 66; Stephen Shames/Visions, 40; UPI/Bettmann Newsphotos, 15, 30.

O

Printed in the United States of America.

1 2 3 4 5 6 7 8 9 10

Library of Congress Cataloging-in-Publication Data   Meltzer, Milton, 1915–   Poverty in America.

Bibliography: p.

Includes index.

Summary: Examines the nature of poverty in America, its effects on children, women, the elderly, and racial minorities, and past and present efforts to fight it.

1. Poor—United States Juvenile literature.
[1. Poor. 2. Poverty] I. Title.

HC110. P6M44   1986   362.5'0973   85-31963

ISBN 0-688-05911-2

CONTENTS

1
MONEY MAKES
A
DIFFERENCE

Money!

It makes a difference—whether you have it or don't have it. It determines the most basic facts about your life:

- Whether or not you're hungry much of the time.
- Whether or not you live among cockroaches and rats.
- Whether or not you freeze in winter and suffocate in summer.
- Whether or not your teeth are rotten.
- Whether or not you get decent medical care.
- Whether or not you can take a vacation.
- Whether or not you can buy the clothes you need.
- Whether or not you go to college.
- Whether or not you're prepared for a well-paying job.
- Whether or not you can afford to marry.

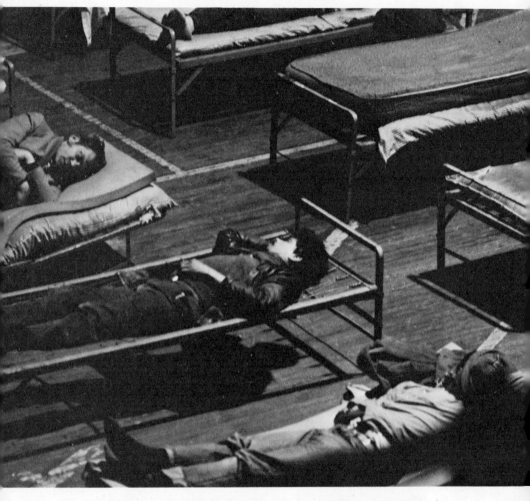

One sign of poverty in today's America: the swelling tide of newly homeless people. Some leave the streets at night to sleep on cots in armories. Come morning, they are back on the sidewalks.

How many Americans don't have money? How many live in poverty? The government in Washington says there are about 35 million people in poverty (out of a population of 235 million). Many experts say there are far more. They say the government's measure of poverty is not accurate and understates the facts. A number of experts say that closer to 50 million people are poor.

Whether there are 35 or 50 million people who are considered poor in this country, these are huge numbers—so huge it is difficult to visualize the actual people behind the numbers. However, they are very real men, women, and children. Here are some snapshots of a few of them:

Mary Smith is twenty years old. She was laid off from a secretarial job in Minneapolis eighteen months ago. Unable to find work, she lost her apartment and had to sell her furniture. She lived on yogurt and water for a month. One night she went to a hospital waiting room and, without anyone seeing her, slipped into an empty bed. When a nurse found her, she sent Mary to a shelter, where the homeless are given a bed and their meals. "It's very scary to be like this," Mary said.

Esperanza Valencia is the wife of a farmworker in California. She is the mother of eight children and expects a ninth. The Valencias live in the Sonoma Valley, where they work in the fields and vineyards when there are jobs. At one time the family lived in a little one-room shack for which they paid $180-a-month rent. It had no stove to cook on, the drains didn't work, and the place was overrun with vermin. Then a sanitation inspector came around and boarded up the shack. So the Valencias lived in their car for five months. When they were able to get work, they were paid $400 a month. It was often hard to feed a family on what was left after the rent was paid. So now they eat beans and tortillas for breakfast, lunch, and dinner. They can't afford milk or fruit or juices. The children come home from school hungry. A Food Bank run by private charity gives them boxes of food now and then. Often that is all the Valencias have to eat.

Michael Kelly is a fifty-six-year-old X-ray technician. He lost his job in a Los Angeles hospital and returned to his hometown of Oakland to look for work. For the first six months there, he lived on the street. His "home" was under a tree beneath the Freeway, a home he shared with many other jobless people. He stood on the breadline at the Salvation Army for the free food it handed out. At first the line wasn't very long. A year later it often stretched for two blocks or more, and women and children were on it, too. Kelly served in the Marine Corps for seventeen years and saw action in war. "I never expected to live like this," he says, and job prospects, he adds, get worse and worse for a man going on sixty.

Leroy Madison, twenty-nine, lives in southeastern Kentucky. He served in the Army for four years, then worked in a coal mine for six years, until he was laid off a year ago. He is married, and his wife is pregnant. The family's only income is $100 a month in food stamps. In return for the stamps, supplied by the federal government to the needy, grocery stores provide food for that amount. The stamps last only the first three weeks of the month, and then the Madisons go hungry for the last week. They pay $50 a month rent, which Leroy Madison works off by doing chores for his landlord at $2 an hour. Mrs. Madison, who is eighteen, gets prenatal care at the Mud Creek Clinic whenever she can get there. She worries about the birth of the baby and how they are going to pay for it. They have no medical insurance.

Nancy McCartan, thirty-seven, worked for five years as an executive of a national computer firm. She left to become part owner of a new computer company in Pittsburgh, but the company failed. Unable to pay her rent, she moved to a much cheaper place without a stove. Her only income was from doing odd typing jobs. Often she lived only on rice and water. She lost thirty pounds within a year. She kept sending out résumés but got no work because people considered her overqualified. Desperate, she called the Hunger Action Hotline in order to be able to eat.

Cynthia Smith, thirty-four, is a single black woman who lives in Aliquippa, Pennsylvania. She got an associate degree in data processing from a community college. Unable to find work in that field, she took a job as a guard at the Pittsburgh airport. After two years she was disappointed in the dead-end job, and went to Cincinnati to look for better work. She lived off her savings for five months, couldn't find work, and went back to Pittsburgh. For about a year she was helped by welfare programs, but then a new ruling cut her off. Her only aid now is $75 a month in food stamps. To get by on it she eats only one meal a day.

Ms. Smith had gone to school to get out of the trap of her childhood poverty. "When I was growing up with ten kids in the family," she said, "I knew hunger then. My mother always taught us that if we wanted anything we would have to go to school and work for it. This is how I was brought up. And so I sacrificed and went to school and worked hard, and now I'm right back where I started in my childhood . . . Now I know hunger all over again. I'm just living, just existing, wondering day upon day exactly how I'm going to survive. My mother went through that, I saw her do that, and I didn't think I'd have to grow up and do that."

These lives are painful to read about. But what is happening to Mary, Esperanza, Michael, and the millions of others concerns all Americans. These are our fathers and mothers, our brothers and sisters. In this democratic society we think of as humane, we are responsible for one another. As citizens, what we do or fail to do about poverty matters to us all.

This brief book will try to show why that is true, and to answer some important questions: Who are the poor today? What are their lives like? Why are they poor? What are their prospects for climbing out of poverty? Is poverty something new or has America always had poor people? What does our government do to help the poor, and how well has it worked? Can we as individuals do anything?

As we go along, I'll take up certain ideas many people hold about the poor: That people who are unemployed can always find a job if they really want one. That the poor like living on welfare and want to keep doing it all their lives. That America spends billions on welfare and job programs but nothing good ever comes of it.

Finally there will be a discussion of the people who are working to eliminate poverty and the organizations that are devoted to making life better for all.

2

TAKING
THE
MEASURE

The poor people whose lives we've just glanced at in Chapter 1 are not unusual—much as we may find that hard to believe. It runs against the American dream we were all raised on. "America is a land of promise and plenty for all," it's often been said. Work hard, save your money, strive for a goal, and you'll win success. That's been true for some. But not for all. Not for many millions. In today's world it's much harder to shape your own destiny. We're often victims of forces beyond our control.

It's easy not to see those victims. We are blind to how our neighbors live. A veil is drawn over their lives. The poor are not the movers and shakers, not the celebrities whose stories fill the newspapers. *People* magazine does not go out of its way to report the daily doings of the poor. The voices of the prosperous dominate the

*House Backs Gradual End
Of Long-Term Jobless Aid*

20 Million Hungry People

*Family Faces Grim Life
As Jobless Benefits End*

*Despair Wrenches Farmers' Lives
As Debts Mount and Land Is Lost*

Study Finds Poverty Among Children Is Increasing

Foreclosures on Homes Rise

Poverty Worsening in City, Study Finds

Experts Doubtful About Outlook for the Poor

*New Midwest Protests Erupt
Over Problems on the Farm*

Families on Aid Juggle
Bills and Money to Live

The Poor:
American Outcasts

Families on Aid Juggle
Bills and Money to Live

In City Quarters, Parents Struggle
To Feed the Youngest Homeless

Warning Over Ignoring
Pupils Living in Poverty

*House Backs Gradual End
Of Long-Term Jobless Aid*

On the Death of Poor Babies

High Death Rate Persisting for Black Infants

news as they have always dominated history.

Yes, sometimes you do find stories about the poor in the papers or on TV. But generally it is when their lives erupt in horror or tragedy. A fire roasts alive the dwellers in a slum tenement. A killing occurs in a desperate family. A baby is gnawed by a rat. A hopeless mother commits suicide. These are moments when the poor become fleetingly visible to middle- and upper-class America.

There are other times when the nation suddenly becomes aware of poverty, of deprivation, of hunger. In 1984–85 mass hunger in Ethiopia roused America's generous impulse. And funds poured into the relief agencies to save thousands from starvation and death.

But millions in the United States are hungry, too. They aren't starving in a dramatic enough way to arouse the same generous impulses that hunger in Ethiopia did. A well-to-do majority thinks of poverty and hunger as something happening in Ethiopia or India or Guatemala, rather than in California or Minnesota or Alabama . . .

Well, what exactly is poverty? And how is an American defined as poor?

To find the answers, it is necessary to know how poverty is measured. Back in the early 1960s, the government decided it needed some way to measure poverty. The experts started with surveys showing that families generally spent about one third of their incomes for food. Then they computed the cost of the cheapest foods that would meet the minimum standards of nutrition. They multiplied the total price for the food by three to take care of other goods and services a family needs—rent, clothing, utilities, transportation, medical care, etc. (I should point out that you can tighten your belt on food, but the other costs are fixed.) If a family's income fell below this final figure—the poverty line—then the family was considered poor. Forty million people, or 22 percent of the population, were poor, according to that first estimate.

The basic measure of poverty has followed this formula ever since. The only changes that have been made since have been annual adjustments of the poverty level because of changes in consumer prices. The latest poverty-level figure, set for a family of four, was given in 1983 as $10,178 a year, or just under $200 a week. But Americans don't agree with this figure, according to a Gallup Poll taken in 1984. They believe that a family of four needs at least $300 a week to make ends meet. So the public perceives living costs to be 50 percent greater than the government says they are.

In recent decades many experts, agencies, commissions, and foundations have studied poverty. They do not agree on how to define it. Is poverty an absolute or a relative condition? It's not an abstract argument. What is decided has a great effect upon the poor and how the government treats them. For instance: if there is an absolute dollar figure for the poverty line, such as $10,178, then a slight shift of that figure up or down greatly changes the numbers of people defined as poor. And the federal funds spent to help the poor shift with the number of people the government designates as poor.

Poverty as a relative condition was defined by the economist John Kenneth Galbraith. He said, "People are poverty-stricken when their income, even if adequate for survival, falls radically behind that of the community." Another writer, Peter Townsend, suggests that "poverty ... is the lack of resources necessary to permit participa-

tion in the activities, customs, and diet commonly ap-
proved by society." He and others claim that the poor are
poor because they lack not just cash income, but legal
services, public amenities, basic human respect, and so
on. They are deprived of the ordinary activities of everyday life—they can't take a vacation, can't eat a meal in a
restaurant, can't give their children a birthday party. So
poverty, he would say, is not an income level; it is a condition of life.

The anthropologist Charles A. Valentine writes: "The
primary meaning of poverty is a condition of being in
want of something that is needed, desired, or generally
recognized as having value." There are variable degrees
of it. "Starvation, death from exposure, and loss of life
due to some other total lack of resources are the only absolute forms of poverty."

Valentine veers toward Galbraith in his conclusion.
Both agree that "the basic meaning of poverty is relative
deprivation. The essence of poverty is inequality. The
poor are deprived in comparison with the comfortable,
the affluent, and the opulent." Most of us when we hear
the word "poverty" think of inequality of material
wealth. But other lacks go with that. In America it's
widely admitted that the poor are deprived of other
things of value—occupations, education, and political
power, to name some. (We will come back to this later.)

It seems, then, that poverty is not a condition of absolute want. You could say it's "having a lot less than most
people," and that could mean having "enough to get by."
You could also say that if poverty is relative, then the
growth of our economy alone wouldn't wipe out or neces-
sarily reduce poverty. The only way poverty could be re-

duced would be to redistribute all the income of the entire nation on a more equal basis.

The federal government, as we've seen, measures poverty as an absolute number which changes only with inflation. This way, the number of poor drops in times of economic growth, and it rises when unemployment goes up, or there is rapid inflation or a recession. This absolute view of poverty makes it possible to change the numbers of people who are defined as poor without changing the way income is distributed.

There are many criticisms of the way the government defines poverty. The present method, however, because it's been the same for some twenty-five years or more, permits us to see trends in the number and percentage of people who are poor. This is how poverty rates have changed in the past quarter century:

From a high of 22 percent in 1959, the proportion of people living in poverty declined steadily to its lowest level of 11 percent in 1973. It stayed very close to that level until 1979, when it began to climb each year, reaching 14.4 percent in 1984, the last year for which there are figures. That's an increase of nearly one third in just four years, a rise which added 9 million people to the number living in poverty.

But the overall rates tell only part of the story. Being poor means many things. One of them is hunger.

3

BREADLINES AND SOUP KITCHENS

Who doesn't know what feeling hungry means?

After a long day at school, you can't wait to get home and raid the refrigerator. Maybe you stop on the way to buy a candy bar or a hot dog. If dinner is late getting on the table, you feel grouchy and snappish and bark at your sister or brother. Watching TV after your homework is out of the way, you start munching snacks washed down with cold milk.

That's being hungry the way most people know it.

It's very different from the hunger that is an everyday fact of life for millions of Americans. They're hungry, hungry all the time, hungry because they are too poor to buy the food the body needs. For people who've never been underfed, it's very hard to imagine what it's like to wake up hungry, to be hungry all day, and to go to sleep at night still feeling hungry. It's a slow death, not visible

Laid off from his job in a Cleveland factory, a worker and his family eat in a soup kitchen run by the Salvation Army. State-funded unemployment benefits usually run out after 26 weeks. A federal program for supplementary payments, which provided 8 to 14 more weeks of benefits to jobless workers, was killed in 1985. Millions of the unemployed go hungry.

to the untrained eye. But the lack of food takes its toll on life all the same.

Dr. Robert Coles of the Harvard University Health Services has studied malnutrition and starvation in the United States and in other places. He describes what happens to a body deprived of nourishment: "The body is slowly, in a sense, consuming itself," he said. It takes in carbohydrates, enough to keep the person going, and yet not enough protein. The body becomes very vulnerable "to all kinds of illnesses which hover over all of us all the time. So what one finds is a severe kind of malnutrition with weakening of the body, diseases cropping up, definite shortening of life."

How much of this kind of hunger is there in the United States today?

At least 20 million Americans now suffer from hunger. It has spread like an epidemic across the nation.

This is the conclusion of the Physicians' Task Force on Hunger in America. The twenty-two-member study group included prominent doctors and public-health experts from across the country. In 1984 the group toured the United States, traveling the back roads, opening refrigerators, searching out what they called "the human face of hunger." The physicians' group reviewed earlier studies of hunger, and then carried out several hundred interviews and field studies in eight states and four regions. The members visited clinics in areas of poverty that reported cases of Third World diseases such as kwashiorkior and marasmus, the result of advanced malnutrition. They also found vitamin deficiencies, diabetes, lethargy, "stunting," "wasting," and other health problems traceable to inadequate food.

The task force found that, despite a recent economic upswing, "hunger is getting worse, not better." Members of the physicians' group saw growing lines at soup kitchens and food pantries, learned about increases in infant mortality, and heard widespread testimony about malnutrition among the unemployed, infants, and the elderly.

In order to reach its conclusion that there are 20 million hungry Americans, the task force used statistics from the Census Bureau and the U.S. Department of Agriculture. It defined hungry people as those who are chronically unable to buy an adequate diet, as well as people who periodically run out of food altogether. The task force reasoned that the 15.5 million Americans with incomes below the official poverty line who do not receive food stamps are unable to get an adequate diet for at least part of each month. They added to that number Americans living close to but not at the poverty line who also do not get food assistance. They concluded that in the United States there is a total of at least 20 million hungry people.

Some of the very old, too, were discovered to be hungry—like those people in Mississippi whose local doctors scolded them for not eating what they couldn't possibly afford. Their poor-paying jobs—maid, yardman, and so on—had not been covered by Social Security, so they get no old-age pension. When their food stamps run out, they go hungry till next month comes around.

"People like these," comments a *New York Times* editorial, "are familiar figures in food banks, soup kitchens, and cheese lines. Some administration officials think they're fakers. But as a man who waited hours for his loaf of processed cheese said, 'Do you think we'd stand in line all day if we weren't really hungry?' "

Close by the White House and the Capitol there is a food kitchen that fed 175,000 hungry men, women, and children in 1984. At costly French restaurants nearby, the tab for one meal can come to more than $100 (a meal that can be written off the taxes of an executive). In the alley, out of sight, the hungry dig into garbage cans for leftovers.

Confirming the findings of the Physicians' Task Force, the U.S. Conference of Mayors states that hunger is "the most prevalent and insidious problem" facing the cities today. Robert G. Kaiser of the *Washington Post* suggests a reason: "The poorest 40 percent of the population (that is, the poorest 100 million Americans) has been earning a steadily declining slice of the economic pie in recent years, while the wealthy classes have been getting much fatter slices." He thinks the fact that things have actually been getting worse for lower-income people runs counter to the beliefs of high-income, powerful people at the top. Mr. Kaiser thinks the rich and powerful prefer to shut their eyes to the truth and shrug it off.

In its report the Task Force on Hunger suggests it knows what has gone wrong:

> The recent and swift return of hunger in America can be traced in substantial measure to clear and conscious policies of the federal government. Hunger is an example of much that can go wrong in Washington. Problems get looked at in terms of Washington, in terms of politics, and not in terms of people. Some political leaders deny the obvious fact that hunger exists because it does not fit their ideological framework. More sensitive leaders rec-

ognize that there is hunger, but avoid intellectual dishonesty about its seriousness, pointing with pride to the few, halting steps they have taken to address it.

Political "reality" and the niceties of consensus politics permit otherwise decent leaders to discuss limited responses to a growing crisis even as the crisis worsens. It is easier to gain acknowledgment of hunger in other nations than it is to do so at home where we are more directly responsible.

Admittedly, we are not politicians. But as a group of doctors and health care professionals, we believe it is time to stop avoiding the problem of hunger. Americans neither deserve to be hungry, nor do they deserve leaders who permit hunger to exist.

As a remedy the physicians called on Congress to:

- Increase welfare and food-stamp benefits and ease eligibility requirements.
- Restore free and low-price meal programs to the schools.
- Expand the nutrition program for women, infants, and children.
- Offer more meals for the elderly.

Second Harvest, the organizer of food banks, does what it can to overcome shortages in government aid for the hungry. It solicits food from national companies and channels it to more than seventy food banks nationally. A juice company in New York, for instance, had three hundred cases of apple, pineapple, and cranberry juices gathering dust in its warehouse. The dented cans could not be sold, although the juices were drinkable. The cases were trucked to a warehouse, and the next day the juices were being served at the Manhattan Church of the Nazarene, where the hungry come daily for meals.

A food bank called Food for Survival collects food items from about one hundred companies each week, stores them in its huge Bronx warehouse, and distributes the products to more than 260 feeding programs in New York City. This system prevents the waste of food while it provides nutrition for the hungry at soup kitchens, food pantries, and emergency shelters. In New York City alone, about 200,000 people a month were being fed through the efforts of food banks in 1985. Other cities maintain the same kind of program.

The donating food companies benefit from getting rid of their surplus, slightly damaged, or unsellable items. They also cut down on or eliminate storage, inventory, and disposal costs. And as the food banks are charitable, any donations by a company are tax-deductible.

Poverty is the root of hunger in America, and as we have seen, hunger leads to illness. Recent medical research shows that heart disease is far more likely to kill poor people than the rich. A study of death rates from heart disease reported it was higher in poor neighborhoods of Los Angeles County than in wealthier ones. And higher among poor blacks than among affluent blacks. Earlier, researchers had found that the poor are less likely to get regular medical checkups, to have medical insurance, to be able to afford health care, and more likely to delay in getting necessary medical treatment.

The situation has worsened since recent restrictive changes in Medicare and Medicaid regulations. Reduced funds have cut the services local health-care agencies can provide for the poor.

Hunger exerts a harmful stress on its victims. The poor feel the strain of constantly scrambling for food. The shame a man or woman experiences over the inability to provide for his or her family adds a terrible burden that increases the physical damage done by poverty. Everywhere the Physicians' Task Force went, it heard the voices of depression, failure, and despair. An unemployed steelworker in Houston told of going to sleep at night and not wanting to wake up. In Peoria a jobless farm equipment worker said he seriously considered suicide because he could not face being unable to feed his kids. Poverty, hunger, illness, death ... Is it a chain that cannot be broken?

4

LIVING
IN THE
STREETS

Under bridges, in doorways, beside boxcars, in parks, tents, emergency shelters, subways, abandoned cars, they seek shelter.

They are today's homeless.

Two to three million people in the United States have no place to call home.

They are white, black, Hispanic, Native American, and foreign-born. They are people in trouble, victims of job layoffs, of greedy landlords, of cold bureaucrats, or of their own addictions or personality disorders. They are abused wives and cast-off children, evicted families, lonely old people. They are among the 35 to 50 million Americans who are poor.

How did the homeless end up on the street? Loss of jobs is the major reason. Another cause is the loss of social benefits. Many physically or mentally disabled peo-

One of New York's many thousands of people living on the streets makes his home on a bench on Fifth Avenue, just across from the elegant Plaza Hotel.

ple who qualified for Supplemental Security Income (SSI)—a program for the aged, disabled, and blind—have been told they are no longer eligible for help. Many more families of the working poor who got supplemental Aid to Families with Dependent Children (AFDC)—a cash program—have been cut from the rolls or had their benefits sliced.

There are rigid requirements for these programs, and when these requirements are not fulfilled, recipients are dropped from the programs. For instance, if a sixteen-year-old in an AFDC family drops out of school, he or she is excluded from government aid. Many young people leave home to make it a bit easier for their families.

When food stamps, Medicaid, and nutritional and social services are cut, people have to use the money they set aside for rent in order to meet these other needs. And then they lose their housing.

"Gentrification," the process by which poorer city neighborhoods are improved for the use of the middle and upper classes, drives many people onto the streets. Families living in cheap apartments or disabled people in single-room-occupancy hotels are forced out by landlords who want to convert the space into high-cost dwelling units. The city rarely troubles to find affordable housing for the displaced people, and federal low-cost housing programs have all but disappeared. The victims of gentrification must beg for shelter with relatives or take to the streets.

Two sociologists from an Ohio college, Marjorie Hope and James Young, drove across the country and talked to the homeless wherever they found them. Most of the homeless they met on the road were made up of two branches of the "new poor." Some had been pushed out of the middle class, and others had always lived on the edge of the poverty line until some force plunged them below that level.

From the middle class come recent additions to the new poor: victims of factory shutdowns. The *Los Angeles Times* describes them as "middle-class families fleeing the dying industrial areas of the East and Midwest" for the Sun Belt. Many are "families with young children ... Recently arrived from Poughkeepsie, N.Y., Charles and Donna Larson aren't used to seeking public assistance or to dining with their two-year-old daughter, Stephanie, in soup kitchens. After two weeks of unsuccessful job hunting in North County [a San Diego suburb], the $250 the family arrived with is gone, and the Larsons are bound for downtown San Diego in search of temporary shelter."

Larson says, "We came here trying to find a better life, and I thought with all my work experience, we'd get on our feet real quick. It didn't work out that way. This is very strange for us."

Of the new poor who had lived close to the poverty line, the Ohio sociologists had this to say:

> These "new poor" had always had insecure jobs as waiters, gardeners, maintenance men, nonunionized factory hands, assistant mechanics, assistant carpenters, assistant electricians—and other assistants. "I can do anything," we heard over and over. But unlike the tinkers of another era, these people had no societal status. Marginal though they were, our companions held "middle-class values": they were clean, neat, and polite; they even refused offers of food. With bravado they spoke of the next job. Most of them disliked sleeping in missions or in

shelters, which they associated with "bums." Instead they slept under the stars, in bus stations, at truck stops, or—when they had a few dollars—in run-down hotels. From time to time they used missions for showers, or as a last ditch. Always they made a careful distinction between themselves and hoboes. They would rather risk the dangers of being robbed by a motorist or being jailed for hitchhiking than the perils of being jammed together with the roughriders of the rails . . .

Life on the streets is compounded of fear, frustration, and boredom. Fear of freezing to death or of torrential rains that can be as bone-penetrating as the cold. Fear of younger homeless men who prey on old men and on women. Among teenagers, fear that authorities will pick them up and send them back to the unhappy situation from which they are running away. For almost all of the homeless, fear of the police . . .

What does it feel like to be cast adrift? Marjorie Hope and James Young describe what they learned from talking with scores of the homeless:

Frustration hounds those who line up at welfare offices, only to be told they haven't filled in the fourteenth page of a fifteen-sheet form, or that the worker can't answer their questions . . . It hounds those who stand in line for an hour or more, sometimes in the rain or snow, to get a meal in a soup kitchen. It dogs those who spend their days hunting for an unpoliced spot to put their heads down to sleep, or a place where they can defecate in private. Perhaps nothing destroys one's dignity more than having to relieve oneself in an alley.

Boredom: What does one do with a day that seems to stretch out indefinitely before one? Only a few cities have drop-in centers where one can retreat from the elements, shower, wash clothes, and watch television. Passersby seem to look through one. Companions are often too exhausted to talk. A sense of worth disintegrates. Even if one has never drunk before, one drinks now, in order to be able to absorb a little more cold and discomfort and harassment, to soften the edges of hopelessness. One drinks to feel that one is somebody.

There are several kinds of shelters for the homeless. They are run by missions or churches or the local government, and some are supported by a mixture of church, public, and private funds. Some offer the homeless very little help or are a hell that many, especially the older and weaker, can't live in. They feel safer on the street. Other shelters are true havens. Most of the mission shelters are concerned with saving souls, not with the social or political reasons for homelessness.

Not many cities provide public shelters. Among those that do are Boston, Chicago, New York, and Washington. New York City had nineteen shelters in 1985. Each provided beds, meals, social services, and medical help. Every night about 7,500 men and women stay in them. The shelters were started because concerned citizens fought for them. Sometimes the shelters are in armories or empty schools, and often they are run by a church group on contract to the city. Shelters directed by church groups may get grants or technical aid from the community. In some cities local taxes are used to pay cheap hotels or private shelters to lodge the homeless.

Some people believe the federal government should take complete responsibility for housing the homeless. Others, like the Catholic Worker movement, believe big government is harmful, that true charity comes not from taxes but from changing people's hearts and minds. They believe that if private families took in just one homeless person, we'd need no shelters or welfare systems. The Catholic Worker has sponsored their own houses of hospitality for the poor.

Conservatives tend to insist that homelessness is really the problem of the mentally ill. Twenty years ago the mental health experts took the view that patients belonged in communities, not in institutions, and that with the help of new drugs patients' behavior could be controlled through occasional daytime visits to neighborhood mental health centers. Huge numbers of patients were discharged from mental institutions without any plan for outpatient treatment or even for housing and SSI benefits. They now wander the streets. Put these ill people back into asylums, the conservatives say, and that will be the end of the homeless problem.

But there's plenty of evidence that many of the homeless are not mentally ill. Of course alcoholics and the mentally ill or physically disabled are a small part of the homeless population. However, it's wrong to say that the homeless and the mentally ill are one and the same. Homeless people are really an extreme result of poverty. The numbers of homeless rise because poverty increases. Economic pressures on the poor and near-poor get worse, as the cost of housing shoots higher and higher, the supply of low-income housing continues to shrink, and the federal government cuts off aid for cheap housing. The gap widens between the shelter people need and the shelter they can afford.

These are real people, huddled in doorways. They need care and housing.

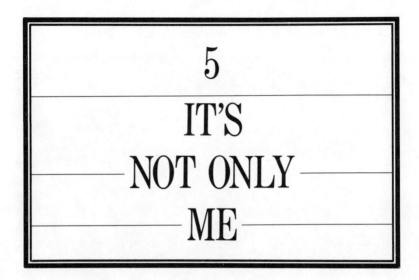

5
IT'S
NOT ONLY
ME

For fifteen years he worked at the Jones & Laughlin steel plant in Pittsburgh. Then, in 1982, Fred was laid off. Nearly three years later, he was still out of work. His unemployment benefits ran out. Married, with two daughters, Fred said he didn't know what would happen to him now. His wife works, mostly part-time. She fills vending machines for $3.75 an hour. He gets food stamps, and his trade union food bank supplies the family with some staples. Now and then friends give him odd jobs to do. "It's not only me," he told a reporter. "It's thousands of other guys."

Not thousands, really, but millions. In the two recessions that have struck America within the past few years, 5.1 million experienced workers lost their jobs. About three out of five got work again. But of those who found

Detroit workers line up to register for state unemployment benefits. The auto industry and its suppliers have been heavily hit by job losses in recent years. Even when production goes up, automation takes the place of many workers. Service and clerical jobs have not replaced the lost manufacturing jobs in significant numbers.

full-time jobs, nearly half were earning less than before they lost their jobs. Many others found only part-time work. And about 2 million, like Fred, are still unemployed and looking for work, or they have given up hope and dropped out of the labor market.

At the beginning of 1985 there were 8.5 million people in the United States looking for a job who couldn't find one. That's 7.4 percent of the labor force, a figure which does not take into account those who have become so discouraged that they've stopped looking for work.

The unemployed are just about everywhere—in the cities, in the small towns, on the countryside. In Connecticut the largest brass producer shut down in March of 1985. About 600 people were laid off. At its peak, during World War II, the brass industry centered in Waterbury gave work to 20,000 people. Today it employs 1,500 workers. The city's three largest brass factories have all gone out of business. They blame their troubles in part on cheap imports of brass.

In the little mountain town of Hot Springs, North Carolina, 435 workers lost their jobs in 1984 when the Melville Shoe Factory closed its doors. Soon a third of the town's retail businesses folded, and now the rest just barely scrape by.

Hot Springs' troubles are typical of small towns throughout the rural South. Only a generation or two ago manufacturers moved South to take advantage of the South's cheap land, its nonunion labor, and its low taxes. These industrialists made shoes, tires, electric motors, automobile parts, and textiles. Today hundreds of these plants have closed. They couldn't stand competition from cheaper foreign-made products.

Take textiles. In one year, 1984, at least 61 textile plants closed in North and South Carolina alone, and the industry dropped nearly 30,000 workers. The two states record the lowest number of textile workers in forty years. Third World competitors have proved they can do better what the South used to do in the past—provide large pools of cheap labor without government restrictions. "The Third World has out-Southed the South," as one Mississippi historian puts it.

What will happen next? Southern textile producers say they plan to meet the competition by big spending on plant-modernization programs. This will bring about a more efficient industry—but it will employ fewer workers. Attempts to attract new businesses to the South have not drawn them in. State officials fear that federal government plans to cut back or wipe out rural economic development programs—such as those run by the Appalachian Regional Commission or the Tennessee Valley Authority—will make a bad situation worse.

It feels like the 1930s again. Large numbers of unskilled workers are once more displaced, just as that other generation was in the Great Depression. The situation doesn't promise to improve. Economists project a drop of 14 percent in the number of manufacturing jobs in the South by the year 2000. Whatever new job openings there may be, they will no longer be in manufacturing. The same trend can be seen nationally—away from manufacturing and production and toward service jobs. For a rural work force that has never been well educated, it is not a happy prospect.

Move the focus to the Midwest now for a closeup view of economic disaster: to Detroit and the whole state of

Michigan. During the 1970s there were huge losses in auto sales because of the gasoline crisis and the swift rise in sales of foreign cars. The bad times went on terribly long. There were so many thrown out of work that there was a dizzying leap in the number of people who needed emergency food, shelter, and medical aid. Detroit went into an official state of emergency, and the state issued a special hunger proclamation. Three out of seven people in Detroit lived below the poverty line in 1980; by 1984 it was one out of two.

A third of the people in the city of Detroit and one out of every seven people in the state were getting some form of public assistance in 1984. Though the auto industry has been making gains in sales recently, there is still high unemployment.

Kentucky offers another example of chronic unemployment. In southeastern Kentucky people depend almost entirely upon the coal industry. All the mining counties have double-digit unemployment rates. The worst-off miners live in Letcher County; its jobless rate is 28 percent. One half the members of the United Mine Workers in the state were out of work in early 1984, and a majority had run out of unemployment benefits.

Visiting Kentucky to survey the economic picture, a Senate committee talked to several mining families. Among them they found the four Hunter brothers, all in their twenties, who had been laid off at the mines. Three of them lived in a small converted camper and the fourth in a windowless shack nearby. Their only source of income was $75 a month in food stamps. They had no medical insurance coverage. Here, as throughout the state, the investigators met hunger and malnutrition.

During the recession of the early 1980s, more than half the workers in this country who were laid off did not get their jobs back when the recession was over. Permanent unemployment reached the highest percentage recorded since the 1930s. A record 4.5 million people were classified as long-term unemployed or discouraged.

A new class of Americans—those who had never known hunger before—had to face that prospect for the first time, a time when federal help became ever more grudging and stingy.

It's a bleak forecast for millions of American workers in economic distress. The National Planning Association says that the United States can expect to face chronic unemployment throughout the 1980s. Even if economic recovery reduces overall unemployment, says the NPA, some groups of workers will be left stranded. They will find no jobs or will receive wages too low to lift them out of poverty.

It is clear that what America faces is a job crisis that involves more than unemployment itself. There are really four aspects to a job crisis:

- Large numbers of people out of work.
- Large numbers of part-time workers who want full-time jobs.
- Large numbers of people working at jobs below their skills.
- Large numbers of people in jobs that don't pay decent wages, but wages that keep them close to the poverty line.

Of course the worst off are the unemployed. To be out of work is more than an economic disaster. It can do great damage to the self-respect of the person who has lost a job or can't find one.

⇝ If you haven't a job, you can't afford the food, the rent, the medicine, the clothing that you or your family need. When that failure to provide goes on long enough, it does something to the way you feel about yourself. You get to think you're not much good, you can't pull your weight, you've failed your family. You feel that you're outside the real world of work and haven't any part in it. You hear people say, "Anybody who isn't working, it's his own fault." Maybe they're right, you begin to think, maybe there's something wrong with *me*.

There are some forms of help available to people who have nothing to live on. Unemployment insurance, for example, is paid to workers who are insured and lose their jobs. They get the benefits (the sum varies from time to time) for a period of weeks. The money comes out of payroll taxes paid by the currently employed and their employers. (It is part of the nation's social insurance program that includes Social Security and Medicare.) Sometimes, when there is heavy unemployment, the government extends the period of benefits for a number of additional weeks. Sometimes it cuts that extra period.

Food stamps, on the other hand, are distributed to the needy alone. Specified standards of poverty must be met to qualify for food stamps. The government sets the rules, which are sometimes loosened or tightened, thereby increasing or reducing the number eligible for the stamps. This is called a "means-tested" program. Such means-tested help—whether in money or stamps or other resources—is narrowly restricted to particular classes of the

poor—the destitute aged, the disabled, and single parents
and their children.

The programs popularly called "welfare" distribute
cash payments. In 1974 these programs were combined in
the federally administered Supplemental Security Income (SSI) program.

Even if a poor person gets some help—unemployment
benefits, food stamps, welfare—this doesn't ease the sense
of personal failure, failure to support a family, failure to
make something of oneself, failure to produce anything
useful. Everybody wants to "be somebody," rather than a
"nobody."

The harm done by unemployment shows itself in many
other ways. The rate of mental illness rises. The strain
drives some people to suicide. The tension brings on family quarrels, alcoholism, child abuse, divorce, and even
higher rates of infant mortality.

There are human beings behind those statistics, those
percentages. They suffer their own self-doubts, and some
face the open or silent criticism of others in the family for
not being good providers or perhaps for the shame of
having to accept welfare.

So being out of work harms the jobless, and at the
same time, it hurts society as a whole. The unemployed
don't have wages or salaries on which to pay income
taxes. They have little to spend, so sales-tax revenues go
down. When factories close, this puts a dent in revenues
raised by commercial property taxes. At the same time,
every person unemployed requires greater government
spending for unemployment benefits, food stamps, welfare, and other aid programs.

Crime, too, is a heavy social cost of joblessness. The

Federal Bureau of Prisons reports that the prison population goes up when available jobs go down. Other studies show links between the jobless rate and the frequency of homicides, robberies, larcenies, narcotics arrests, and youth crimes. More crime means greater costs for courts, prisons, police, and hospitals.

But the greatest cost can't be measured. It's the talent that is wasted, the skills that wither, the creativity that's lost, the hope that dies.

What accounts for the critical job shortage in the United States?

There's no one simple answer, but some of the reasons are quite plain.

To step back a minute, the number of jobs in a society relates to the size of the population, the country's resources, and the pattern of consumption. When the population goes up and consumption increases, so should the number of jobs. That has been the general pattern in this country. However, a few times since World War II the labor force has increased while the number of jobs declined. That caused high unemployment.

Several things can upset the balance between population and jobs. One is automation, which is the replacement of workers with machines and/or advanced technology. That has seriously cut the number of jobs in many industries. To name a few: textiles, crude-ore mining, sugar manufacturing, auto production, aluminum production, copper manufacturing, farming.

Another factor that contributes to unemployment is industry's practice of cutting back to keep production in limited or even short supply, and thus to keep prices high. Even in boom times 10 percent of all American factory production is idle. In slumps, a third of all industry can be idle.

A third factor is the importing of cheaper products from abroad. Unable to meet the competition, American factories reduce production or shut down plants.

A fourth factor is the decision of many American industries to move their factories to foreign countries. Thus they avoid U.S. taxes and reduce their labor costs. This causes severe job losses.

A final factor in recent times has been the federal government's intervention on the economic front. The administration decided to stimulate the job market by giving businesses extra tax breaks, hoping that business investments would increase, and the result would be more jobs. Critics say it hasn't worked out that way. Business often pockets the extra profits from the tax breaks and doesn't increase production. New jobs aren't created in significant number.

America clearly needs more jobs if unemployment is to be ended. But no one is sure how many jobs are needed and how to create them. Surely there is nothing "natural" or "necessary" about putting people out of work and keeping them there. Conservative estimates hold that if we are to get rid of poverty, we need to create an additional 10 to 12 million jobs and to upgrade 20 to 30 million other jobs. More liberal estimates say that perhaps 50 million jobs will be needed over the next decade.

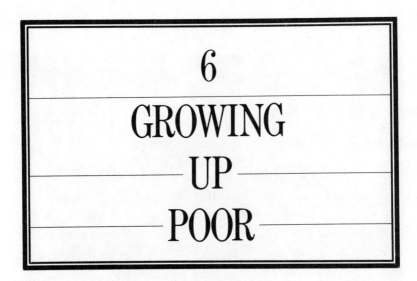

6
GROWING
UP
POOR

With their four children, Billy and Veronica Fontaine live in a beat-up old car. At six every morning the family drives to a public recreation area so they can all wash and use the bathroom. They wouldn't have anything to eat if it weren't for Evelyn Taylor, the principal of the children's elementary school. She arranges free hot suppers twice a week for some eighty children and their families. She also runs a Food Bank at the school and has organized big giveaways of clothing donated by the district's four hundred teachers.

This is in San Mateo, California, where the students of North Shoreview Elementary School who are poor have little to eat and not much to wear. They sleep in cheap motels or their cars. Most of these families are on welfare and can't afford apartments on the money they get from

Children make their home in an abandoned building. They are part of the growing number of Americans under 18 who live in poverty. One out of five children— nearly 14 million—are poor. For many the solution to poverty is running away. While the number of poor children has grown, the amount of government aid to them has dropped by one-third. More American children die from poverty than from traffic accidents and suicides combined.

the welfare agency. When they pay the motel bill, no money is left for food or clothing.

Nearly half of all poor people are children. Today one of every four American children under the age of six and one of every two black children under six are poor.

Growing up poor means having to do without. Your parents have trouble paying the rent. They can't buy you shoes or jeans. When they can't meet the payments, the men come to take the refrigerator away. The hard facts color every aspect of life for both you and your parents. You feel pain, fear, anger, loneliness. You live in a world you have no control over.

Dr. Robert Coles, studying the life of the poor, was told by a mother how her children feel:

> Now, they'll come back at me, oh, do they, with first one question and then another, until I don't know what to say . . . They'll be asking why, why, why, and I don't have the answer, and I'm tired out, and I figure sooner or later they'll have to stop asking and just be glad they're alive.
>
> Once I told my girl that, and then she said we wasn't *alive,* and we was dead, and I thought she was trying to be funny, but she wasn't, and she started crying. Then I told her she was being foolish, and of course we're alive, and she said all we do is move and move, and most of the time she's not sure where we're going to be and if there'll be enough to eat. That's true, but you're still alive, and so am I.

The poor children in America have parents who are perhaps an unemployed steelworker or auto worker or miner. They have parents who may be farmers gone bankrupt. They are the children of the single parent who gets little or no child support and who works at a minimum-wage service job. They are the children whose family broke up in divorce, and now they live with Grandma, who struggles to get by on Social Security.

The poverty rate for children is consistently higher than for the general population. And it's been getting worse. About twenty years ago, nearly one out of every eight persons under eighteen was poor. Now it's one in five. If the child lives in a family headed by a woman, it's still higher—more than one out of four. In male-headed families it's one out of eight. (In New York City it's even worse—one of every three children lives in poverty.) With female-headed families increasing rapidly, the prospects for the children in those families are bleak. However, when bad times come, as in recent years, even two-parent families and their children join the poverty ranks.

If you're a teenager and poor, the best chance for a decent future is to find a job. But for teenage Americans, the unemployment rate is 50 percent—a record high. Unable to find work, thousands of young people take up lives of hustling and crime, which many are likely never to leave. It's one reason that street gangs are on the rise in the cities.

In making a study of the job problem for young people, the sociologist William Kornblum talked to many teenagers from poor neighborhoods. One of them was Vincent P., a fourteen-year-old black living in the poorest section of Cleveland's East Side. Vincent is in the eighth grade, the right place for his age. He had done well in school until recently; now his reading and math scores are slipping. This is from Kornblum's report:

———————

In talking with Vincent, we hit on a subject that immediately sparks his interest—work and his experiences attempting to make money. "I love trucks and driving," he says. "When I get older, I want to drive a big steel-hauling rig like you see coming out of the mills." Vincent continues to describe how his close friend Eugene and he often take long walks into the industrial areas of Cleveland, where they discuss the big machinery and the work men do with those machines.

"I used to work on a truck with my father," Vincent continues. "We'd drive all the way to Georgia and load up the truck with watermelons, and then we'd sell 'em all in two or three days right here. Sometimes we'd load up with junk and things out in the country and sell it to the used-furniture stores. I love driving trucks and loading 'em up with stuff." As he talks, a sadness overtakes him. In painful fragments he goes on to describe how his father was shot to death in a senseless family dispute when he was thirteen years old. Since then, his mother has remarried. The stepfather is kind and helps him as best he can, but Vincent misses his father and that truck.

The pain Vincent is experiencing is clearly affecting his schoolwork, but he is such a quiet and easily forgotten child that no one outside his immediate family pays much attention to him. He would like to grow up to be a long-distance truck driver or a "steel-mill man like my uncles before their mill shut down."

Vincent is like the great majority of poor young people in the ghettos who are failing in school. Yet if they got some help, they could become productive citizens. In New York City alone there are over 200,000 unemployed school dropouts. A small fraction of them make money in illegal hustles they wouldn't trade for minimum-wage jobs. The others, however, would respond to job openings made for them in the larger society. If only attention were paid to them in the critical time of their coming to maturity . . .

Recently in Massachusetts the state public health department reported that nearly one in five of the low-income children it surveyed was either stunted, abnormally underweight, or anemic. Similar results have been found in many other places. The Children's Defense Fund, a private agency, concludes that "poverty is the greatest child-killer in affluent America."

Governor Mario Cuomo of New York points out:

> We have more single-parent families than ever before. More women in poverty. More teenage mothers without a proper education or the prospect of a job. We have increasing numbers of children whose mental and physical development have already been stunted by poor nutrition and inadequate medical care.

Most parents of poor children have no medical insurance and don't have the money to pay medical bills. Less than half of these children are immunized against such preventable diseases as measles, polio, and diphtheria.

A group of noted physicians, sponsored by the Field Foundation, visited Mississippi to find out at firsthand what poverty and hunger did to children's health. In their report they said:

> We saw children whose nutritional and medical condition we can only describe as shocking—even to a group of physicians whose work involves daily confrontation with disease and suffering. In child after child we saw: evi-

dence of vitamin and mineral deficiency; serious, un-treated skin infections and ulcerations; eye and ear disease; also unattended bone diseases secondary to poor food intake; the prevalence of bacterial and parasitic disease; as well as severe anemia, with resulting loss of energy and ability to live a normally active life.

The children described in this report lived in a state in the Deep South several years ago. But the same poverty and hunger, found anywhere or at any time, will produce the same sad effects. It is proof of how crucial the right amount and kind of food is to a child during his or her formative years. It acts upon the child in almost the same way that programming does upon a computer. The baby's life is patterned from those early days.

If you aren't poor, it's hard to imagine what it's like to be born hungry and stay hungry. *Born* hungry? Yes, hunger for many children starts when they are still in the womb. The pregnant mother who is poor can't afford to eat the well-balanced diet needed to maintain her vitality and assure the baby's normal development. If the unborn child suffers severe lack of nutrition, it can be damaged for life. This result is easily explained. The adult brain weighs about three pounds and consists of some 13 billion cells. Ten billion of these cells are developed within the first five months in the mother's womb. Those billions of cells must last for the rest of life. If injured, they do not grow back or mend; nor do they reproduce. In the last few months of pregnancy, the brain develops rapidly in the womb. After birth, the brain's growth slows down, coming to a stop at about age five.

If the mother is poor, the unborn child gets too little protein and other nutrients. And in many cases the brain is stunted. The baby is permanently handicapped. If the mother remains poor, the baby is not likely to be fed properly during the first five years of life, when the brain can still grow. So the child comes to maturity with brain power significantly below normal.

Poor nutrition of the pregnant mother is also the major cause of premature birth, which then cuts down on the time the baby has to grow in the womb and increases the chances of a baby entering the world with a permanent handicap.

So malnutrition and a lesser chance for good health are passed from the hungry mother to a hungry infant.

Babies born underweight are the most vulnerable to death, disease, and starvation. If newborns weigh 5.5 pounds or less, they are most at risk of dying during the first four weeks after birth. In the United States about 6.8 percent of all babies are born underweight, a worse record than in at least twelve other developed countries. If the underweight babies survive, they are more likely to suffer serious diseases and congenital conditions such as cerebral palsy, mental retardation, seizures, and problems of vision. Poor nutrition in the pregnant woman is one of the most basic causes of low birth weight, as are smoking, drinking alcohol, and taking drugs.

There is a direct link between parents out of work and infant mortality. A study in Allegheny County, Pennsylvania, where steel mills shut down and thousands of workers lost their jobs, showed white infant mortality tracked closely with the rate of unemployment during the 1970s. The mortality rate for black infants was 19.6 in 1982. That's twice the rate for white infants. Unemployment for blacks and Native Americans is considerably higher than for whites.

The effect of economic inequality is plain again in figures from Minnesota. There, infant mortality rates for blacks and Native Americans were two and a half times that for whites in the three-year period of 1979–81. If a child was unlucky enough to be born in a low-income neighborhood in Minneapolis, the child's chance of surviving infancy was only half that of a child born in a more affluent neighborhood.

7

WOMEN IN THE JOB GHETTO

There is a new phrase in the press nowadays. It's the "feminization of poverty." It means that women have a harder time than men when it comes to staying out of poverty. There are many reasons why.

One is that the number of families headed by women has shot way up in the past twenty-five years. For many women, poverty begins when their marriage ends. Half of all marriages in the United States today end in divorce. One in six families are headed by women who have to support children. For minorities the figure is even more startling. Women head 50 percent of all black families and 19 percent of all Hispanic families.

Payments for child support amount to very little. About 40 percent of divorced fathers contribute nothing to their children's upkeep, and those who do were paying an average of $2,100 a year in 1984. That is scarcely $6 a

A young mother opens the "door" to her family's home, made from plastic sheets in a tent city along the San Jacinto River in Houston. Children living with a mother in single-parent families are four times more likely to be poor than those in two-parent families. Because of sexual discrimination, women have a much harder time than men making a living.

day, which buys very little food. So the woman who must both raise and support her children must earn a family wage.

There is "feminization of poverty" because women's pay is generally low. Women who work outside their homes full-time and year-round earn only 59 cents for every dollar men earn. So having a job isn't itself the cure for poverty among women.

Yet more and more women, both married and single, are taking jobs. Over half the women of working age are now in the labor force. The trouble is, those jobs are mostly in what's been called "women's work"—clerical, retail sales, service. And these "female" jobs are dull, low-skilled, and pay less than most males earn. These jobs are often part-time or temporary, provide limited benefits, and offer little status or chance to advance.

This isn't the impression you get from the slick magazines. They play up the two-parent family where both partners work in high levels of business or in the professions. But of all employed wives, less than 1 percent are in the elite professions such as doctor, lawyer, professor, architect, or scientist. And in the business world, only a handful of women reach the executive level.

The truth is, 60 percent of employed women work in only ten occupations, all with poor prospects for enabling them to live decently or develop their natural skills and talents. In addition women suffer outright discrimination. Wages, salaries, job classifications, promotions—in none of these do they get an equal break with men.

What do these facts mean for children? About one in every five children in this country is now living apart from one parent. Because of increasing divorce rates, separations, and out-of-wedlock births, it's estimated that nearly one of two children born today will spend part of his or her first eighteen years in a family headed by a single mother.

The traditional American family, in which Mom stayed home while Dad worked, is coming to a fast end. Many millions of women are now single mothers with at least one child under five years of age. What happens to the child? Only 15 percent of these women have their children in day-care centers. That's true for two reasons. There are nowhere near enough centers to take care of the vast need, and poor working women can't afford them anyhow. There are 6 or 7 million little children without any preschool or afterschool care, and millions more with informal and often substandard arrangements for child care. Almost no industrialized country in the world, for that matter, provides day-care facilities for working mothers of dependent children. The possible exceptions are Belgium, France, and East Germany.

What about older women? They make up a sizable segment of the poor. Seventeen percent of all elderly women live in poverty. Of women over sixty-five who live alone, more than half are poor. A quarter of all widows have gone through all the money their husbands left them soon after their husbands have died. Yet the average widow lives eighteen years after her husband's death. These women can't look to private pensions for help because their jobs, if they ever had any, tended to be low-paid and without a pension. Few widows collect on their husband's pensions. Social Security benefits help, but they are relatively small, and 60 percent of those who do get Social Security have no other income to supplement it. The poverty rate for married persons over sixty-five is quite low. It is 8 percent, less than half the rate for the rest of the population. Social Security works well if two people share a home.

What chance does a woman have to get out of the job ghetto of "women's work"?

In the professions, women lawyers and doctors are doing somewhat better than they were fifteen years ago. That's true for women in skilled blue-collar jobs, too. But these gains for a small fraction of educated or trained women don't hold for the mass of women. Their average earnings have in fact gone down slightly. And even if the economy should enjoy boom periods again, it doesn't mean women's occupational prospects will improve. There are two reasons for this.

The first is that the country's economy is shifting from basic manufacturing (steel, auto, rubber, etc.) toward service and clerical jobs. Since the early 1970s most new jobs have been in fast foods, data processing and other business services, and health care. The service-providing companies now account for 74 percent of the jobs in the United States. These are tagged women's jobs, and the work is badly paid, dead-end, and unproductive, as has been shown.

The other trend has to do with increasing automation, especially in the new microelectronic technology. New technology lends itself to turning skilled jobs for men into less skilled jobs for women. Even skilled work for women gives way to less skilled work. The unskilled operator takes over from the machinist; the clerk with a computerized inventory system takes over from the department-store buyer; the word-processor operator takes over from the secretary.

The result? Fewer men can earn a wage that supports a family. And more and more women, married or single, will probably be poor and remain poor, whether or not they are employed.

Unless some things change.

Just to remind ourselves of what the main things are: One is the fact that society places on women the major burden for child-rearing (for which most women do not get paid). What women can earn and how far they can advance is further limited by the way society fences them into inferior jobs and then discriminates against them on the job.

8

HOW
THE
ELDERLY LIVE

A new stereotype about America's elderly has swept the nation. It pictures carefree, healthy old people rushing out of their Florida condominiums every morning to play eighteen holes on the golf course.

This stereotype has replaced a previous one, which lumped senior citizens into a homogeneous mass of frail, poor dependents. The truth is somewhere in between.

There are many old people across the nation who are still poor. In 1982 the figure was nearly 4 million elderly living at or near the official poverty level, which was set at nearly $5,000 per person a year. That was not nearly enough to buy life's necessities.

Bill Parham, a gear-cutter in Detroit, thought his savings would provide a modest retirement for himself and his wife when he had retired and was no longer earning

Older citizens, organized as the Gray Panthers, demonstrate for changes in government policies to meet their needs. At least four million elderly live in poverty. If not for the Social Security program, the number would be far more.

money. But those savings were eaten up by steep climbs in heating bills, by inflation, and by illness. James Light, a black man in the same city, worked thirty-two years for a small company with no pension plan. He, like many other blacks, was discriminated against on the job market, forced to take menial work, and paid in cash under the table. So there were no Social Security benefits when James Light and others like him retired.

How do these retired people live now? They go hungry, said Father William T. Cunningham, director of Focus: Hope. He was testifying before the Senate Special Committee on Aging:

> Hunger in Detroit is desperation. It is old people in restaurants ordering a cup of tea at an uncleared table and furtively eating leftover scraps of french fries and sandwiches. It is opening and eating from packages of cookies or cold cuts on the supermarket shelf while pretending to shop. It's seventy-five-year-old Annie Harris, full of pride and dignity, confessing that after her last trip to the hospital for starvation, she would have killed herself if she did not believe in Jesus.
>
> Hunger in Detroit is constant worry. It's worrying whether the partial loaf of bread, the remnants of jam, and the last box of macaroni and cheese will take you through three days until the Social Security check arrives. It's dropping the same teabag in hot water for the second day. It's Robert Lindsey, eighty-one, teased with the question of what he would do with more food, saying, "That's beyond my comprehension." Hunger is a forced choice between a carton of milk and a roll of toilet paper.
>
> Hunger in Detroit is guilt. It is old people who won't

tell you their children's names because they don't want to
be a burden. It is the guilt of sons and daughters who
have to abandon their parents because in today's economy they can hardly feed their own children.

And hunger in Detroit is anger. It is old people saying,
"They treat us like an old horse, only they don't shoot us,
they just starve us inch by inch. They've got the food, but
they just won't give it to us." The anger of old people is
quiet despair, knowledge that the refusal of food is a final
rejection, that one's fate is a lingering, lonely, fearful, and
disregarded wait for death.

The Social Security program has made a great difference
for the elderly. In its more than fifty-year history, it has
shown that it works. Growing rapidly in the 1970s, it cut
the poverty rate among the elderly from about 35 percent
in 1959 to 12.4 percent in 1984. If we had no Social Security, over half the elderly would be poor.

Since 1974 the poverty rate of older citizens has re-
mained fairly stable. This is because automatic cost-of-
living adjustments have worked as planned. They protect
the elderly from the damage inflation brings. When the
cost-of-living adjustment (called a COLA) is frozen, as
has happened, it can push more than half a million below
the poverty line.

It used to be rare to see an American eighty-five or
older. In 1900 there were only 123,000 such people. By
1980 they numbered 2.3 million. And by 2050 the eighty-
five-and-older group is expected to be 16 million people,
or 5 percent of the total U.S. population. Many of those
eighty-five and older are poor. There is almost double the
rate of poverty over the age of eighty-five than among

those over sixty-five. Among those eighty-five and older, more than 20 percent had incomes lower than the poverty level in 1983.

So as the population ages and lives longer, the poverty rate for older people seems bound to increase. Unless, that is, retirement benefits improve and government policies do more to prevent or reduce poverty.

9
WHEN
A
FARM DIES

Thousands of small and mid-sized American farms failed in 1985. Farm families that had worked the land for generations were pitched into poverty. Fear and despair spread among hundreds of thousands of farmers who foresaw the loss of millions of acres and watched their neighbors' farms fall into the hands of creditors.

What has happened in American agriculture is that the traditional family farm has been sacrificed in the name of greater efficiency. The number of U.S. farms has declined steadily since 1935. It is expected to drop another third in the next twenty years. According to the U.S. Department of Agriculture, there were about 2.5 million farms in the United States in 1980; by the year 2000 there may be only 1.8 million.

Big companies are taking over farming while large debts and falling land prices drive the smaller farmer out

After 18 years struggling to make a living on their
Illinois farm, the Noll family is forced to see their land,
equipment, and home sold at auction for a considerable
loss. Thousands of American farms have failed in recent years, pitching rural families into poverty.

of his old way of making a living. When the smaller farms fail, it usually means that the larger farms expand. Back in 1969, the top 1 percent of farms received 16 percent of national farm income. By 1982 that thin top layer had expanded its take to 60 percent.

Only size and wealth seem able to protect the farmer against the uncertainties of a market influenced by a great many forces—domestic and international—outside agriculture. For those who are not among the giants, survival is the big question.

"Everyone's having problems," said Mrs. JoAnn Forsness. She and her husband raise beef cattle and alfalfa on their farm in northeastern Montana. "You can't sell things lower than what it costs to raise them," she told a *New York Times* reporter. "We're going broke along with everyone else."

Because of financial problems, the state's agricultural department reported that 45 percent of Montana's farmers expected to be out of business within five years. They are among the nation's 2.2 million farmers who are having trouble paying high interest rates on their borrowings. Many farmers are quitting, giving up the land; others are obliged to turn their land over to their banks after years of struggle against rising debts. For lack of credit many are unable to buy what they need to plant when the season starts. In Iowa's rural counties high rates of suicide are reported.

In North Dakota the Mental Health Association holds workshops to help farmers suffering from the stress of their myriad problems. The counselors see much marital discord, child abuse, and alcoholism. Mrs. Beth Wosick of the association says there's a grieving process when a farm dies. It's like the grief after a suicide. People ask, "What could I have done? What didn't I do?" People whose farms were foreclosed—taken by the bank because they couldn't pay their debts—said they didn't want to go on living. The suicide and divorce rates have gone up. When credit problems hit, marriages fall apart. People just give up.

Crowds of farmers drown out the auctioneer to halt foreclosure sales in the farm states. In St. Paul a crowd of 10,000 arrives in caravans to give Minnesota's governor and the legislators a list of their demands. They want state and federal action to ease their economic plight. Everyone remembers the day a desperate farmer and his son killed two bankers in the town of Marshall. In Chicago a nine-block-long march of hundreds of farmers and their wives arrives at the Board of Trade to protest against an unjust marketing system.

A survey taken in Minnesota predicts 13,000 farmers will face foreclosure in the next eighteen months. In Iowa, land values have fallen 37 percent since 1981. It means the value of what farmers already owned in land, buildings, and equipment dropped by $35 billion.

A nationwide study of the farm problem by the Food and Agricultural Policy Research Institute and the *Farm Journal* predicts that, barring a dramatic change in farm income or vast federal aid, by 1988 at least 20 percent of today's farmers will lose their land. The study also warns that it could lead to an upheaval in rural America unseen since the Great Depression of the 1930s.

Farmers in financial trouble worry not only about themselves but about their community. In town after town stores and other small businesses have failed. Merchants go broke when farmers go broke. The small towns are becoming ghost towns.

Mount Ayr, a town in southern Iowa, is but one example. As a result of farm failures, one of the local farm-implement dealers has gone out of business, and one of the two banks has failed. The main department store has shut down. Applications for mental health benefits have tripled. To help farmers cope, seventeen churches offered social services and opened food pantries. Tons of potatoes were sent out to needy farmers in five neighboring counties.

Iowa is a state that produces one tenth of America's food, yet farmers line up at Thanksgiving for free turkey dinners. (It used to be that most farmers had chickens and a milk cow and a vegetable garden. Not anymore.) So many young farm families have been forced off the farm that half the county's 6,000 residents are over sixty. The local farmers have endured several years of floods, drought, farm failures, and bankrupt businesses. Is the worst behind? Some pray it is; others say this is mild compared to what will happen to farmers in the future.

For the large numbers of migratory farm workers poverty is and always has been their common lot. In the 1960s and 1970s Cesar Chavez's United Farm Workers brought better wages and working conditions to some, but the great majority are still exploited fiercely. In California's Imperial Valley, for instance, as many as 8,000 Mexican workers with the "green card" permitting them to enter the United States provide growers with cheap labor. They cross the border each morning between one and three to stand in the street hoping for a labor contractor to choose them. The lucky ones are trucked to the fields for a day's work at rock-bottom wages.

It's a funny world, this world where farmers go broke while people go hungry. Cyndie Tidwell of the Minnesota Foodshare sees it this way:

> It is a confusing and ironic image of America—a nation that had to put nearly one-third of selected croplands in "idle" to try to reduce surpluses of basic commodities, and still ends up "holding the bag," so to speak, with warehouses bulging with excess food—while we here in Minnesota, part of the breadbasket of the world, have hundreds of thousands of our brothers and sisters unable to put adequate food on the table, or to meet other basic needs on a secure basis. We ask if it is possible to say that every person as a member of the community has inherent rights and claims on the resources of the community in a just society. That seems to be an emerging consensus of the community here—and might it not be reasonable to assume that it would also be the consensus of this nation?

We can't say people are hungry because there is no food. In one year the farmers of America grow twice as much food as our country can consume. But while millions go hungry, the government builds bigger barns to store the superabundance. Is it crazy? To let people go hungry, not because there's a shortage of food, but because they can't afford to buy it?

10
THE PRICE
OF
RACISM

Contrary to what most people think, two thirds of the poor are white.

But blacks and other minorities have far more than their share of poverty. The rates of poverty are highest for those groups that have long suffered the most from racial prejudice and discrimination.

Blacks are about three times more likely to be poor than whites. While one out of every eight whites is poor, one out of every three blacks and more than one out of every four Hispanics and Native Americans is poor. The average black family income is only 58 percent of white family income. And that gap has been widening for many years.

If you look at black Americans today, you see both the advances and the setbacks in their conditions. Advances include the victory of blacks in mayoral races—from

Father and son on the steps of their Appalachian home. Black and other minorities suffer far more than their share of poverty. Over one-third of black Americans are poor, and more than one-fourth of Hispanics and native Americans are poor. The gap between white family incomes and minority family incomes has been widening for many years.

Chicago, Los Angeles, Atlanta, Detroit, and other big cities to hundreds of smaller ones. The soaring into space of the first black astronaut. The adoption of Martin Luther King, Jr.'s birthday as a national holiday. The moving up of better-prepared black workers from low- to higher-paying positions. The great gains in the fight for black dignity, self-respect, and identity.

A short time ago, none of this would have been possible. Older Americans cannot forget how hard it has been for blacks to achieve progress. But their gains have not been enough to bring full equality with whites. Millions of blacks—and their numbers are growing—are still living in poverty, still feel hopeless about their future.

The truth is that there is more black poverty than at any time since Kennedy's New Frontier and Johnson's War on Poverty and Great Society programs. How come, when black sociologists say that "significant positive changes have taken place in white attitudes towards blacks"? The reason: long decades of racism have kept an extremely high percentage of blacks poor and unskilled. Even when times get better, many blacks are not prepared to take advantage of the opportunities.

It is ironic that between 1960 and 1980 the proportion of blacks in professional, technical, and craft positions went up from 11 to 21 percent. But the percentage of blacks below the poverty line rose from 31.4 in 1973 to 35.7 in 1983. Black Americans keep sliding back in almost every part of life that counts. The reason for some of this is because of changes in the American economy. The complex forces we looked at in Chapter 5 have made the new American poverty worse. Some of those forces are international. For example, Japan has 18 percent of the American car market, almost all the videotape-recorder market, most of the television-set market, and large slices of the markets for steel, machine tools, microchips, and office equipment. When have you bought a suit or a dress or a shirt that wasn't made in some Asian or Latin American country? The United States buys more goods abroad than it sells abroad. Imports are killing many American jobs. Traditional American industries are fading away, and so are the jobs these industries provided.

These forces have combined not only to keep poor people poor, but to frighten large numbers of people not yet poor but in real danger of soon being poor. The loss of manufacturing jobs is painful for anyone, but blacks are disproportionately hurt by the decay of our industrial centers.

Older blacks suffer a double danger. Not only is their poverty rate considerably higher than that of aged whites, but they have endured racial hardships all their lives, and now old age makes it even worse. A team of sociologists points out this is because blacks bring

> to their older years a whole lifetime of economic and social indignities, a lifetime of struggle to get and keep a job, more often than not at unskilled labor, a lifetime of overcrowded, substandard housing in slum neighborhoods, of inadequate medical care, of unequal opportunities for education, and the cultural and social activities that nourish the spirit, a lifetime of second-class citizenship, a lifetime of watching their children learn the high cost of being a Negro in America.

What about the other ethnic minorities? What risk do they run of being poor?

Immigrants continue to enter the country at a high rate. The Population Reference Bureau forecasts that 800,000 to 1,000,000 people will come in annually all through the 1980s. About half of them enter illegally, primarily from lands to the south. The urge to migrate remains high in the Latin American and Caribbean countries because their young-adult population grows rapidly and there are nowhere near enough jobs for them at home.

The Hispanics come with hope, but many find work only in the underground cheap-labor market. They live in fear—victims of hunger, disease, extortion, and an exploitation often close to slavery. Nearly 3 million of the American poor are Hispanics. The largest group are the Mexican Americans. They live mostly in the West and Southwest. One in four of them is poor. A large number are migrant workers. They tend to have large families, earn much less than the median income, and are less well educated than the average person.

In the Texas port city of Brownsville, for example, a school principal reported in 1984 that 90 percent of his students came to school hungry each day. Hunger cripples the attempt to learn. "In my ten years in the Brownsville system," he said, "I find the problem worse now. Most of it is due to poor nutrition. Our children are seeds for the future. The problem is that we're not watering them."

A doctor in the Rio Grande Valley of Texas who directs a health center has grown bitter about the national indifference to the Mexican Americans he serves:

The majority of my patients wander all over America working the crops. They have no education and poor conditions. They are hungry. Our people have become human garbage. They are damned. I am told that elephants don't die of disease; they die of starvation when their teeth fall out. That is the same thing that happens to my patients.

Mainland Puerto Ricans are the next largest group of Hispanics. One out of three is poor. Only about a fourth are high school graduates. The majority live in the ghettos of New York City. They are generally unskilled or semiskilled workers who are quickly fired when times get bad. Like the blacks, they have seen their jobs vanishing from the cities. They don't have a car or the money for public transportation to follow the factories into the suburbs for low-paying jobs. Nearly 60 percent of all Puerto Rican families are headed by single women. When they work, they earn even less than men.

Cuban Americans are the next largest group. Many from the middle class have adapted readily because of superior education at home in Cuba and have done well. Still, about 14 percent of them are poor.

In recent years large communities of Asians have taken root in many sections of the country. They, too, gather in their own neighborhoods, often in crowded tenements. Many work steadily but at very low wages. Their barriers are job discrimination and language.

As for the Native Americans, who number under one million, the poverty rate is estimated to be 45 to 50 percent. Something like half of all Native Americans live on government reservations. And 90 percent of those living on reservations are said to be poor.

Common to the fate of blacks and other colored Americans is the curse of racism. For the poverty of blacks, Hispanics, and Native Americans society blames heredity, IQ, shiftlessness, immorality. The true trouble lies with racism and the prejudice and discrimination that flow from it.

Racism is the false belief that some "races" are superior and others are inferior. Modern science has proved that no group of people is superior to another. There are simply no innate differences in ability or character from one racial or national group to another.

But racism goes back centuries in America and existed worldwide before the first whites brought it to this continent. The white colonists believed that the colored peoples—the red people and the black people—were inferior, were less than human. It gave them an excuse for enslaving Africans and killing off large numbers of Native Americans. It was convenient and profitable to assert that colored people were good only for doing the hard and dirty work the whites did not want to do.

Over the centuries those racist beliefs were woven into custom, law, education, and religion. Racism was no longer only an act by an individual white against an individual member of a minority. It took the form of the whole white community discriminating against an entire minority. Members of racial minorities became systematically excluded from an activity or function that the larger society believed to be important. Or they were permitted only a subordinate part in it.

It became "natural" and "necessary" to segregate minority peoples and discriminate against them. Jobs, schools, churches, housing, transportation, politics—almost every area of human life was infected with racism. Even the most respected newspapers and journals—from the *New York Times* to *Harper's*—were once guilty of the crudest racism. Articles, stories, poems, editorials, cartoons, jokes by the thousands depicted blacks as stupid, ignorant, dull, lazy, vicious. And similar stereotypes, often with fresh negative variations, circulated about other minorities.

Racism may be less open and less harsh today than in the past. The civil rights struggle and changes in the law of the land have helped make a vital difference. But racism still exists, and its victims are always within its reach. It has much to do with the creation of some of the poverty detailed in these pages and in its perpetuation.

11
THE DREAM
OF
ABUNDANCE

From the very first, immigrants have brought with them to the New World dreams of abundance. Most immigrants came to escape poverty. The life they knew in preindustrial Europe was truly terrible. Before 1720 probably half the people of England never got enough work to do or food to eat. They died early of malnutrition and disease. In London, a refuge for the landless poor, three out of five boys died before they reached sixteen. No wonder the English turned heavily to alcohol, a narcotic against the horrors of daily life. Funds provided by each parish barely kept the poor alive.

In America the immigrants did not have to contend with the rigid social classes of Europe or the mass rural poverty. But from the start many new farmers in the colonies teetered on the edge of poverty. In 1780 Michael

With the Great Depression of the 1930s three years old, the federal government still expected charity alone to ease the suffering caused by mass unemployment. In December 1932, thousands of jobless Americans paraded through the nation's capital to demand federal relief from the Hoover administration. A few months later, the newly elected Franklin D. Roosevelt launched a program to provide jobs and relief.

Gaffney, a rich man of Charleston, South Carolina, rode into the rural districts and reported what he saw:

> The country for about 150 miles from Charleston is extremely low and unhealthy. The people looked yellow, poor, and sickly. Some of them lived the most miserably I ever saw any people live ... Their dress is generally a hunting shirt and some trousers of coarse cotton yarn ... The women of this country live the poorest lives of any people in the world ... They must do everything from cooking to plowing and after that they have no more life in them ...

The settlers who followed the explorers to America didn't expect such harsh conditions. They believed what lay ahead in the New World couldn't be worse than what they left behind. The colonies offered free land, and with the shortage of hands there was a demand for labor. The poor could gamble on the future by exchanging ship passage to America for a set number of years in bonded service. Probably half the white immigrants of the colonial period came as contract laborers. For many the risk paid off. They finished their short-term slavery and became free farmers or workers. Many others found their masters and conditions unbearable. Some fled to the frontier; some could find no way to escape the brutality of their lives other than by suicide. Wherever they finally settled, the immigrants found life in America to be hard and exhausting toil. The poor became "the hands and feet of the rich," as one historian put it.

In the southern colonies the system of bonded servitude provided too few hands to meet the needs of the planters. So slaves imported from Africa became a bitter part of the American history of poverty. The Africans came poor, like so many others, but they came in chains, against their will, and the laws of slavery permitted them no way out of the poverty they were condemned to. Talk of a land of promise and plenty was a mockery for them.

Slavery was a special form of poverty. But the blacks were not alone in their poverty. As the economy of the colonies grew, so did the gap between rich and poor. For each man who might make his small farm or business pay, dozens of others failed.

The public had little mercy for those without work to do. To the whipping post, prison, or workhouse they were sent. "Poor laws" were on the books in most colonies. Taxation provided a dole, small handouts for the needy. As part of the Christian creed, charity went usually to orphans, widows, and those too handicapped to take care of themselves.

By 1750 many farmers whose lands were too poor to support them were coming into the cities to seek a living. Here they competed for work with immigrants just off the boat. Only some prospered. A fourth of the people of Philadelphia were poor in 1772. In New York City, a fifth of the population needed public aid in 1815. Historians think perhaps a fifth of all whites and nearly all blacks lived in poverty as the nineteenth century began.

The public didn't seem to care what happened to the poor. The worst off could enter a "poor farm" maintained by the community and do some work in return for their keep. These places were let on contract, and the men who took them over were seldom merciful or generous. Few people—except for the utopians who dreamed of an ideal communal life—thought of trying to end poverty. The ordinary middle-class person pushed the poor out of sight and out of mind. The poor were poor because somehow they didn't fit in, more fortunate people believed. The community's duty was only to provide a handout.

The first of many economic crises to devastate America came in 1837. Many people had been gambling with investments, and business had grown increasingly shaky. Crop failures in the spring hastened the economic collapse of the country. Mechanics and laborers suffered badly. Prices of food and fuel shot up, and desperate people rioted in the streets. Every third worker in New York lost his job. Ten-year-old boys and girls labored in the mills of New England from dawn to dark at tasks often beyond their strength and pocketed hardly more than a dollar a week.

"See the unnatural contrast in Man's condition," Rev. Theodore Parker told his Boston congregation. "Bloated opulence and starving penury in the same street." Now the poor are deserted by their employers, he said, yet it was their sweat which enriched the ground and built the costly houses and the new railroads. Bread and rent riots erupted on the streets. The effects of the depression lingered for nearly seven years. "Not money, but poverty, is the root of all evil," said the reformer Lydia Maria Child.

As the crisis stretched on, a potato famine in Ireland killed a million peasants and drove another million to America. Instead of being welcomed into the "land of the free," they were shunned by the old-time Yankees, who couldn't believe the new immigrants were really human. The only jobs open to the Irish were the most menial labor. They were condemned to live in shanties and slums. They were denied aid by the various charitable societies. Business viewed the newcomers only as a source of cheap labor on the rapidly developing railroads.

When the Irish began to settle in Concord, Massachusetts, the writer Henry David Thoreau tried to borrow money for a poor Irish neighbor who wanted to bring his family over to this country. In his journal Thoreau noted the common attitude toward the poor:

> One will never know his neighbors till he has carried a subscription paper among them. Ah! it reveals many and sad facts to stand in this relation to them. To hear the selfish and cowardly excuses some make—that if they help any they must help the Irishman who lives with them—and him they are sure never to help! Others, with whom public opinion weighs, will think of it, trusting you will never raise the sum and so they will not be called upon again; who give stingily after all. What a satire in the fact that you are more inclined to call on a certain slighted and so-called crazy woman in moderate circumstances rather than on the president of the bank! But some are generous and save the town from the disinction which threatened it, and some even who do not lend, plainly would if they could.

With an almost fatal rhythm, depression after depression came along to throw millions out of work. Hard times hit again in 1867, in 1873, in 1884, in 1893, and in 1907 ... All were bitter disasters for working people, whether the crisis lasted a year or many years. One of the biggest and most widespread depressions struck in 1873. A New York labor paper, *The Toiler,* reported:

> Thousands of homeless men and women are to be seen nightly sleeping in the seats in the public parks, or walking the streets ... The suffering next winter will be tre-

mendous. Three thousand boys and girls applied at the 6th Ward Station House for tickets for the poor children's excursion; scarcely one of them had shoes or hats, and half were naked . . .

Year after year the depression that began in 1873 went on. By 1877 one out of five workers was jobless, and two out of five worked no more than half the year. Breadlines and soup kitchens pocked the streets. Legions of the unemployed drifted across the country, hunting for work. Workers with steady jobs suffered wage cuts of as much as 50 percent. When a Chicago worker killed himself, a newspaper noted, "No cause, except for despondency caused by poverty, was assigned."

How widespread was poverty? A young man from Indiana, Robert Hunter, tried to answer the question. The son of a manufacturer, he was appalled by the effects of a depression that began in 1893. In 1904, after examining the poor at home and abroad, he published a book called *Poverty.* In it he showed that there were at least 10 million people in America (12 percent of the population) who were "underfed, underclothed, and poorly housed." Only about 4 million of those 10 million poor received any public relief. The city slums were "wildernesses of neglect," as he put it, "almost unexplored and almost unknown," to the people on the upper side of society.

Many families slightly above the poverty line drawn by Hunter had a bad time trying to stay afloat. They usually had scanty furniture and no property. Their small rented flats lacked hot or running water and indoor flush toilets. Bread and potatoes were their diet. Getting sick or losing a job would wipe out their small savings if they had any. They could not fall back on unemployment benefits, public welfare, or old-age pensions because none of these benefits were in existence at that time. Charity distributed by the church or public-spirited citizens' groups was the only help available to the poor, and it was painful and shameful to have to beg for it.

In 1890, just before the depression studied by Robert Hunter, there were 12.5 million families in the United States. Of these, 11 million had an average income of $380 a year. The richest 1 percent of the country enjoyed wealth greater than the total remaining 99 percent. As one scholar said, "Never before or since in American history have the rich been so rich and the poor so poor."

It was a time when the rich could spend $75,000 for a pair of opera glasses and decorate a pet poodle with a diamond collar worth $15,000. Andrew Carnegie, who drew $25 million a year from his giant steel mills, defied any man to show him there were paupers in this country. From his palace on Fifth Avenue he could not see Potter's Field, where the bodies of one out of every ten people who died in Manhattan were dumped nameless into mass graves.

To be sure, there were some among the poor that society called the "undeserving." They were the drifters, the drunks, the irresponsibles, guilty of what the experts termed "personal misconduct." One estimate held that about 12 percent of the poor in the 1890s were in this category. Far more numerous were the dependent people who could not be blamed for their poverty. They were the disabled, the chronically ill, the aged, the women with dependent children. Then, as now, dependency was a major source of poverty.

While poverty persisted, industry grew rapidly. It made

for such abundance that no one thought the country's wealth could ever be exhausted. The rich kept getting richer and piled up the means to invest and become even richer. The corporations their lawyers created soon dominated the oil, electrical, railroad, mining, and many other industries. But by the 1890s social critics realized the aim of these corporations was not to provide plenty for all. No, it was rather to provide superabundance for the few. Monopolies or "trusts" were established by powerful businessmen to control prices in a given industry and suppress competition. Alarmed by such great economic power in the hands of the few, reformers warned that the corporate lords would dominate not only the workplace but the halls of government.

There were feeble attempts to rein in the trusts. But the great trust-buster himself, President Theodore Roosevelt, finally endorsed the claim that making the rich richer means making everyone richer. "In our industrial and social system," he said, "the interests of all men are so closely intertwined that in the immense majority of cases a straight-dealing man who by his efficiency, by his ingenuity and industry, benefits himself must also benefit others."

America came out of World War I as the world's greatest industrial power. Politically, too, it had become the central force in international affairs. In the 1920s Americans felt sure they were the biggest and the best—in everything. Running for the presidency in 1928, Herbert Hoover declared:

We in America today are nearer to the final triumph over poverty than ever before in the history of any land.

The poorhouse is vanishing from among us. We have not yet reached the goal, but given a chance to go forward with the policies of the last eight years, we shall soon with the help of God be in sight of the day when poverty will be banished from the nation.

Hoover spoke for most middle-class people. They thought the American dream of unlimited plenty was close to fulfillment. The Roaring Twenties were a very good time for many of them. Trying to get rich quickly and easily, they gambled on land booms in Florida and stocks on Wall Street. But working people had no extra money to invest. In 1929, of the country's 27.5 million families, 21.5 million or 78 percent earned under $3,000 a year. And 16 million of these families received less than $2,000 a year, which was what social workers and economists called the unofficial poverty level of that time. Among them were 6 million families with incomes under $1,000 a year.

Again, as in the 1890s, the gap between incomes was wide. The 27,500 wealthiest families in America had as much money as the 12 million poorest families. While miners and lumbermen earned about $10 a week, Andrew Mellon was paying an income tax of $1,883,000, Henry Ford a tax of $2,609,000, and John D. Rockefeller, Jr. a tax of $6,278,000.

Unemployment, too, was common in the Roaring Twenties. Layoffs for industrial workers averaged 14 percent between 1924 and 1929. Whole regions of the country knew hard times all through the twenties: the textile towns of New England, the Allegheny coal towns, the Deep South, the shipbuilding and shoe-manufacturing centers of the North, farmers everywhere. The majority of Americans lived at or below a bare subsistence level.

When he entered the White House in 1929, President Hoover announced, "We have reached a higher degree of comfort and security than ever existed before in the history of the world." Six months later the Wall Street stock market crashed. Stock prices plunged sickeningly day after day. As the panic went on, most people could not believe what was happening. The Great Depression had begun.

Many weaknesses underlay the operation of the complicated economic system in this country. Wages and prices, trade and investment, production and consumption, machinery and manpower were not regulated by government and could be thrown wildly off balance. When the panic struck Wall Street on that October day in 1929, it was like the breach in a levee that releases devastating floodwaters.

The Great Depression gripped America—and much of the world—all through the 1930s. At its cruelest depth, in 1932–33, some 13 million people—one out of every four Americans who had held jobs in 1929—were unemployed. The historian David M. Kennedy summed up its effects:

In that age of single-income households and virtually nonexistent welfare programs the real human misery implied by those cold statistics was incalculable. Immigrants by the tens of thousands abandoned the American land of promise and slouched back to their old countries; families went unstarted as pinched budgets and sagging self-esteem wrought a sexual depression in countless American bedrooms; 20 percent of New York City's school children suffered from malnutrition, educators reported; Oklahoma City and Minneapolis were rocked by hunger riots—while, paradoxically, hillocks of unmarketable grain rotted beside railroad tracks across the Plains states. Many Americans might have trembled for their country in 1933 if they had reflected that lesser crises in other places had toppled governments and given birth to tyrants—like Hitler and Mussolini.

Hoover looked to charity to ease the suffering. He believed the government must not give doles. He rejected a program to help farmers who were in deep trouble. He believed in letting the sickness remedy itself. Things would get so bad that they must then get better. His recovery plan was to make government money available as loans to business, believing those funds from the Treasury flowing out to the banks and corporations would then flow back to the people. As the humorist Will Rogers put it, "The money was all appropriated for the top in the hope that it would trickle down to the needy."

The needy didn't believe it would work that way.

It didn't. The stricken had shared in Hoover's make-it-on-your-own philosophy that had elevated him from Iowa farm boy to multimillionaire. But now it failed them. Hoover became a target for bitter jokes as a sense of hopelessness gripped the nation.

In the grim autumn of 1932 Hoover and the Democratic candidate, Franklin D. Roosevelt, campaigned for the presidency. Roosevelt was as hopeful as Hoover was discouraged. FDR promised experimentation and change. He won easily and took office in March 1933.

12

A SAFETY NET– WITH BIG HOLES

Roosevelt acted swiftly, getting from Congress broad executive powers to wage war against the Depression. Called into special session, in one hundred days the Congress passed bill after bill in the hope of bringing about economic recovery. Federal relief for the hungry came first and then billions to provide public works so the unemployed could find jobs at last.

A patchwork of plans quickly improvised by lawyers, economists, and sociologists brought to Washington by the New Deal made a difference. The vigorous intervention of the federal government gave cash relief to many of the jobless, put four million others back to work, gave help to farmers, set up controls to regulate business and finance, protected labor's right to organize, provided a wages-and-hours law, and began a low-cost housing program.

Fifty years after the depression of the 1930s, mass unemployment again plunged millions into poverty. And again Washington saw jobless workers rallying on the Capitol steps for badly needed government help.

FDR had no blueprint for the solution to the country's deep troubles. Most Americans do not think in terms of a single solution. They deal with a problem when it comes up. If a thing that's tried doesn't work, they look at it again and come up with another answer. If that fails, they try something else. Big or small, problems are usually treated that way. Few Americans, then or now, believe in a single solution for all problems. If one were dreamed up, it would probably do more harm than good.

Unemployment, however, persisted throughout the 1930s. It took the menace of Hitler and the war crisis of 1939 to put every employable American to work again in the booming defense industries.

The New Deal did not answer the basic economic question, which is: How can our immense natural wealth and productive potential be made to benefit every person in America? The New Deal shored up the middle class, restored jobs to half the unemployed, and gave just enough in money and jobs and low-cost housing to the lower levels of society to restore good will. What guided FDR and his advisers was the desire for government to intervene in the economy enough to prevent a depression, to help the poor, and to curb destructive practices of big business. Roosevelt was not willing to remake or replace basic economic and political institutions.

Most of the American people expected no more. They yearned to have "normal times" back, even though in normal times millions were "ill-nourished, ill-clad, and ill-housed," as FDR himself put it.

The Great Depression of the 1930s jolted middle-class Americans out of the belief that a decent livelihood came solely from a willingness to work. It wasn't just a few of the handicapped and a vague number of shiftless people who needed help. Millions of people who knew how to work and wanted to work could not find work. The victims were everywhere. The dizzying climb of the unemployment rate to over 20 percent proved that not personal weaknesses but broad economic forces were crippling and destroying lives. As unemployment hit more and more of the middle class, its conviction that the federal government had no business providing support to the poor crumbled.

The poor themselves did not expect much help when the Depression began. Like the middle class, they believed no one had a *right* to a minimum standard of living or even to charity. They didn't think of appealing to their government for aid. They knew there had always been poor people and always would be. The unemployed were too beaten down at first to organize for political action. Social workers pleaded for better welfare standards but without the voice of the poor behind them. It took a few years for the mass misery of the 1930s to create pressure groups among the newly dispossessed.

In response to that popular demand for federal aid, Washington provided the Social Security Act of 1935. It was the foundation on which all other assistance programs proposed since that time have been built. As the first federal effort at income support, it went far beyond the limited local and state programs that existed, with their low funding and narrow coverage.

The New Deal measures recognized that the economy failed to provide enough income to keep people out of poverty. But it did not attack the causes of economic breakdowns. It simply singled out certain categories of people who needed assistance.

The program had four main parts:

- General relief. Funded by the federal government, the states, and localities, it was mainly for the so-called unemployables.
- Work relief. Paid for by the federal government, it was for employables.
- Categorical public assistance. For the needy, the blind, the aged, and dependent children.
- Social insurance. Paid out of private funds, through taxes on employer and employee, it provided pensions for retired workers and temporary benefits for the jobless.

Students of that period agree that the general relief program did not go far enough. FDR wrongly expected that economic recovery would be more rapid. The need was much greater than the federal relief budget provided for. The states and localities did not put up enough money for their share. Local relief officials were often untrained and treated the unemployed stingily.

In 1935 the New Deal turned to a work relief program that would not compete with private industry, would conserve human skills, and would increase buying power. The Works Progress Administration (WPA) was a major advance in welfare. It employed both blue-collar and white-collar workers, including people in the arts and professions. Writers like Saul Bellow, Ralph Ellison, Studs Terkel, Richard Wright, and John Cheever worked for the WPA wage of $23.86 a week. So did artists like

Jackson Pollock, Jacob Lawrence, Romare Bearden, and Willem de Kooning. Later most of them looked back on those times as tremendously exciting years of community, of sharing, of pioneering.

An offshoot of the work relief program, the National Youth Administration (NYA), gave part-time jobs to over 2 million students and another 2.5 million youths who were not in school. Much good was done for the nation by the work relief programs—schools, hospitals, playgrounds, airports, bridges, and highways were built, and millions took pleasure from the plays, concerts, art exhibits, and other entertainment provided by people who recovered their pride and confidence on the WPA payrolls.

Still, during most of those years (1935–40) the work projects helped only about three out of every ten of the unemployed.

The third part of the New Deal's welfare program created aid to the needy over sixty-five, to blind people, and to dependent children. This was a liberal step toward helping the "deserving" poor, those who had no other place to turn. It made aid a federal responsibility but required matching grants from the states. It was the largest such program ever devised with the aim of helping children of divorced or deserted mothers, and it exists today under the name of Aid to Families with Dependent Children (AFDC).

Poverty has persisted, especially with the rapid growth of female-headed families. This has resulted in AFDC becoming the most costly of federal assistance plans. In 1984 that program provided subsistence to 3.7 million heads of households—91 percent of whom were women.

It is the program most often accused of harboring "welfare cheats"—that is, of spending money on people who cheat and don't really need help. Yet there is no evidence that AFDC creates a "welfare class" of people who want to spend their whole lives supported by federal funds. It serves families acutely short of income in some stages of their lives.

Studies show that over 90 percent of all women who received help from AFDC in the late 1960s or the 1970s were in need for relatively short periods of time; they used AFDC to supplement their earnings from work or other sources. Their average time on the program was twelve months. It is clear that most families stay on welfare only if they have no other way to meet their basic needs. Studies also show that "welfare cheating" is minimal. Contrary to popular beliefs, more than half the recipients of AFDC are white, and more than 70 percent of such families have only one or two children.

The enormous pressure of meeting the economic disaster of the Great Depression left few in government with time to probe beneath the surface for the long-range problems. Why had low income persisted during the abundant twenties? Why did millions of hard-working farmers stay poor? Why was income distributed so unequally? Some economic thinkers suggested that the dislocations and malfunctions of the system which produced unemployment and distress were not accidental. Maybe there was something wrong with the very nature of the way the economy was organized. They saw poverty as but one evil in an economic system that got out of control in so many ways and so often.

Such experts urged government to stimulate the economy. They wanted it to promote purchasing power, and they favored a fairer distribution of income. However, their ideas didn't make much of an impression on the middle-class mind. Polls showed a majority of the middle class believed the government had an obligation to aid the "truly deserving" poor, including the newly unemployed. But the old myth hung on that the poor could get off relief if they only wanted to. Jokes about WPA workers and people on welfare were popular. The jokes and myths about the poor made it easier for luckier Americans to conceal their guilt over not helping neighbors in trouble.

The down-and-out had been quiet in the first years of the Great Depression, stunned by the magnitude of the disaster. But anger grew, though it rarely turned into an attack upon the system. Rather it was expressed in blaming the "big shots" in business and the Hoover administration, who had failed so badly or who didn't show they cared. Many of the poor channeled their energy into support for old-age pensions and plans to "share the wealth" by guaranteeing everyone a livable income. Nearly 90 percent in a national poll agreed that "the government should see to it that every man who wants to work had a job."

The unemployment benefits and old-age pensions of the New Deal were giant steps forward. No longer could social benefits be considered handouts by kindly employers. For the first time they were established in law as *rights*. It took a terrible depression to bring these laws into existence.

Why hadn't it happened before? For one thing, the middle class had always been cool to the poor, unable to see themselves in the poor's shoes, confident they would never be in such trouble. As taxpayers, they always worried about keeping costs down. If the money for social services was to come out of their pockets, it had better be as little as possible. And there was that old damning stereotype—that hard work always pays off, and therefore no decent person needed public aid.

The myth goes far back in American life. The celebrated preacher Russell Conwell crisscrossed America in the nineteenth century, delivering the same speech about "making it" some 6,000 times. "Opportunity is in your own backyard," was the message. The religion of success is even older. Cotton Mather, the Boston divine, preached it in colonial times, and the theme has echoed ever since. Right after the Civil War, a timid and lonely Unitarian clergyman, Horatio Alger, began to write short novels about pluck and luck. His heroes, Ragged Dick and Tattered Tom, were hugely popular among young readers. They spoke for a simple faith in hard work and self-improvement as the sure road to riches. If you only worked hard enough, you could not fail. There was no room for social and economic forces in those pulp stories.

The prosperity that followed World War II made it easy for America to ignore the continued existence of the poor. In Western Europe it was different. Those countries suffered enormous loss of life and property during World War II. Out of that experience came a powerful sense of common cause, of helping one another in time of trouble. Britain, France, Scandinavia, the Low Countries—all developed social insurance programs to benefit everyone.

The Scandinavian countries, for example, believed society was obligated to protect its weakest members not only against thieves, murderers, and foreign enemies, but also against economic disaster. Their social programs came out of a fundamental sense of group solidarity. In Denmark these programs cost three fifths the value of what the country produces; in Sweden the figure is two thirds.

This did not happen in the United States. (Our programs are 15 percent of the gross domestic product.) We were lucky to be spared the worst horrors of that war. It was easy for the middle and upper classes to ignore the poverty that continued during the good times. The sick, the old, those too tied down by family duties to get a job, the low-wage and migrant workers, the pockets of poverty in depressed regions—few paid attention to them. The policy makers and the public were only dimly aware that poor people existed. Times were so good! And it was generally thought that economic growth would surely make poverty disappear.

It took one book to shock Americans out of their complacency. In 1962 the political activist Michael Harrington rediscovered poverty in America. In a passionate outcry, *The Other America,* he laid bare the misery of a new poverty that crippled the lives of 40 to 50 million people. His book gradually became a bestseller, winning the attention of many influential people. President John F. Kennedy told his advisers to study the problem. Before he could do much about poverty, the President was dead, and President Lyndon B. Johnson took over what Kennedy had begun and expanded it.

The civil rights movement of the 1960s and '70s helped focus national attention on the fact that there were still millions of poor. They were hungry, they lacked medical care, they were badly housed. The movement's demands and the riots in the cities forced a bigger response from the federal government. Something needed to be done for the poor who did not fit into the categories of the Social Security Act.

So a "War on Poverty" was launched. It was part of President Johnson's drive for what he called the Great Society. People felt confident that the economy would continue to expand, that poverty could be conquered. Some of the milestones that became law in 1965 included:

- Medicare, providing health insurance for the elderly, financed by payroll taxes.
- Medicaid, which pays for health care for the poor.
- Rent supplements for poor people.
- Special development assistance for Appalachia, one of the most depressed regions of America.
- Manpower training programs for youths and adults.
- A Model Cities program to combat poverty in the neighborhoods.

The Office of Economic Opportunity (OEO) was created to run these programs. It funded projects, inspired action, and coordinated it. (The OEO was gradually phased out in the 1970s.)

The War on Poverty was attacked from the right. Conservatives called it "a poverty grab bag." Too many still believed the poor were poor because they were dumb or lacked ambition. Welfare programs are wasteful, they said. "The only solution to poverty," wrote a conservative columnist, "is free enterprise and continued economic growth—those things which made America great."

Twenty years later few of those critics would deny that

Medicare and Medicaid and several of the other measures have been a success. They provided a safety net for
the poor. The fears of those in Congress who voted
against the measures were not borne out. America did not
become a socialist state. Government spending for social
programs continued and increased markedly in the Re-
publican administrations of Richard Nixon and Gerald
Ford. Welfare eligibility rules were eased in Nixon's time.
Food stamps and Supplemental Security Income for the
aged and disabled became national programs. Millions
more became entitled to Medicaid. And most important,
Social Security benefits were set to rise automatically as
inflation pushed up the cost of living.

The antipoverty program never gave poor people what
many of them needed most—a regular, decently paid job.
Instead the programs provided for specific needs. They
gave the hungry food stamps. They gave those unable to
afford medical care Medicaid. They gave the ill-housed
some public housing and rent subsidies. The programs to
meet specific needs were neither seen nor sold as something designed for all citizens. Only for the poor, and in
the eyes of many, chiefly for black people.

The War on Poverty programs were created in a time
of business expansion and didn't seem to Congress too
costly a burden. However, because of lack of funding, the
programs proved to be not a "war" on poverty but only a
skirmish. Less than 1 percent of the federal budget was
spent on this "war" in any given year of the 1960s. Then
in the late 1970s and early 1980s the economy stalled and
stopped growing. Budgets were hastily reviewed. Money
had to be saved, the mounting national debt cut back. It
was easy to slice programs targeted for the poor. They

were a minority, without political clout. People who got food stamps were labeled cheats. The image of the woman with a full shopping cart buying steak was fixed in the public mind as the typical food stamp recipient. See, you can't give things away, because if you do, people will take advantage of you. Such people don't want to work, they just want to live off the government. Thus the nonpoor get to feel morally superior to "those people." And ready to accept attempts by a President or a Congress to cut down on such benefits for the "undeserving poor." But we've seen throughout this book how genuine the needs of the poor are, and how big the holes are in the safety net that is supposed to keep them from drowning.

It's worth noting that not just the poor but the well-off get many benefits from the government. However, the poor are clearly visible. Food stamp recipients must show their stamps in the grocery store every time they need to eat. Medicare recipients must carry their cards. People in public housing live in big projects everyone knows are for the poor. The goods, services, and subsidies the poor receive are out in the open for all to see. It's natural for us to conclude that only the poor get help.

Who is aware of the great variety of government programs that help the *non*poor? A casual list includes price supports, acreage allotments, low-interest loans, tax breaks and loopholes, government purchases . . . Every one of them subsidizes the income of many millions of the nonpoor, including huge corporations and the truly wealthy.

Look at the corporations, for instance. According to Citizens for Tax Justice, a private research group, 128 of the 250 most profitable corporations paid no taxes at all or received rebates in at least one of the first three years of President Reagan's administration. This happened despite these corporations' total profits of $56.7 billion. The five leading defense contractors—General Electric, Boeing, Dow Chemical, Tenneco, and Santa Fe/Southern Pacific—paid no income tax for three consecutive years in the early 1980s. General Dynamics, one of the biggest defense contractors, has paid no income tax since 1972, yet it made a total profit of $2 billion from 1972 until 1980. Such benefits are not visible to the general public, and it is not apparent that the government is giving away such huge sums to the already rich. Contrast the low visibility of the corporate tax subsidies to the high visibility of the food stamp program.

It is not common knowledge that Social Security benefits were reduced by $100 billion between 1981 and 1985, while corporate tax subsidies in 1984 alone totaled an estimated $90 billion, excluding the defense budget.

13

WHAT CAN BE DONE ABOUT POVERTY?

Too many Americans are poor, while too much of the nation's wealth belongs to the rich.

This situation is a grave challenge to the way the economy works and raises such questions as what does the imbalance between rich and poor do to people? To *all* people, both rich and poor? Does the economy enhance or degrade human dignity? Does it give everyone a chance to share in the work and life of the community?

A committee of American Roman Catholic bishops recently drafted a pastoral letter that examines these questions.

The draft calls for a new common agreement that "all persons really do have rights in the economic sphere and that society has a moral obligation to take the necessary steps to ensure that no one among us is hungry, homeless,

Where to go? What to do? How to live? A homeless,
unemployed man passes the endless empty days and
nights on a cot beneath a California viaduct.

unemployed, or otherwise denied what is necessary to live in dignity."

This is not the first time religious groups have studied the question of poverty and injustice. In 1982, Methodist Bishop James Armstrong, president of the National Council of Churches, urged an approach much like the Catholic bishops. Thousands of years ago, the Hebrew prophets of the Old Testament showed a special concern for those whose human rights had been most often abused. Echoing those passionate voices, the ecumenical Center for Theology and Public Policy has declared, "We are to bear good news to the poor, release captives, give sight to the blind, liberate the oppressed, proclaim the arrival of a new order of love and justice."

More and more, the churches are becoming involved in poverty and the economy. In the Monongahela Valley of Pennsylvania, when the U.S. Steel Corporation closed plants or cut the work force to a small fraction, ministers from twenty congregations attacked that action as "institutional evil." They urged the corporation to invest in communities with mass unemployment, rather than to invest their funds overseas. These corporations "cannot continue to place profits before people," said the Rev. D. Douglas Roth of the Trinity Lutheran Church in Clairton, where employment at the local steel plant dropped from 6,000 to 1,200 workers. "We are saying that you just can't put people in the street and destroy people for profit."

In Rome, Pope John Paul II in December of 1984 condemned the arms race and the gap between rich and poor nations. The money spent on arms, he said, "could be used to alleviate the undeserved misery of peoples that are socially and economically depressed." He added that "an unfair distribution of the world's resources and the assets of civilization" has created "a form of social organization whereby the distance between the human conditions of the rich and the poor becomes ever greater. The overwhelming power of this division makes the world in which we live a world shattered to its very foundations."

In February 1985 thirty-six prominent religious leaders urged Congress to commit itself to end poverty in the United States. "Poverty in this country can and must end," their statement said. It was signed by leaders of major Protestant and Jewish denominations, religious agencies, and ecumenical organizations. "Out of our faith grows the conviction that no one, child or adult, should suffer the debilitation of poverty," the statement went on, citing the pastoral letter of the American Catholic bishops. "We must seek justice; we must protect the vulnerable."

"Antipoverty programs comprise less than 10 percent of the federal budget," the statement said. "Even so they have borne nearly one third of all budget cuts adopted in the past four years . . . Funding for programs for the poor has neither caused the deficit nor threatened the stability of the economy."

As we write, the administration of President Ronald Reagan is in its second term in office. To reduce poverty the administration has relied on a growing economy that it believed would improve the well-being of all Americans by creating jobs. For those unable to provide for themselves, the Reagan administration has stated that the federal and state governments must maintain public assistance programs to assure every American a decent standard of living.

But in its annual budgets, the administration has made heavy cuts in programs for the poor such as food stamps, AFDC, and Medicaid, although these cuts were sometimes modified by Congress. Broader programs not targeted at the poor, and which make up four fifths of federal social spending, received much smaller cuts. Yet the administration has made little effort to withdraw the special tax breaks and other subsidies flowing to middle- and upper-income households.

When President Reagan began his campaign to reduce federal spending, he said he was counting on "voluntary strength" to carry on some of the social services the government had provided. Corporate giving to charity has increased in recent years, but "it has come nowhere near filling the gaps left by the Reagan administration's cuts in government support of social programs," reported the *New York Times* in 1985.

Is there a better method than depending on charity and the government to help the poor? Some program that could achieve a more equitable distribution of income? Many public interest organizations and policy research groups have put forth such lengthy proposals that it would be difficult even to highlight the most important in this book. However, the Catholic bishops' pastoral letter calls for a redistribution of wealth, and we will examine this proposal. Its ideas come from materials provided by a wide variety of specialists who appeared before the bishops' drafting committee.

The program discusses employment first. It says that a

job with adequate pay should be available to all who seek one.

To that end, it recommends:

- A major new national policy commitment to full employment.
- Increased government support for direct job-creation programs. These can be developed in the public sector or through subsidies to private industry.
- Expansion of apprenticeship and job-training programs supported jointly by business, labor unions, and government.
- Improvement and expansion of job-placement services on both the local and national levels.

Full employment would eliminate or greatly reduce poverty. Until that is achieved, the poor must be helped. The Catholic bishops urge all citizens to do all they personally can to alleviate poverty. The letter proposes a national strategy to deal with poverty. It includes:

- Building a healthy economy to provide jobs at a decent wage for all adults able to work.
- Removing barriers to full and equal employment for women and minorities.
- Changing the tax code to eliminate tax burdens on the poor.
- Fostering self-help programs among the poor.
- Encouraging schools to develop policies leading to higher-quality education for poor children.
- Making improved child-care services available to working parents through government funding, tax benefits, and employer-provided day-care services.

Turning to welfare reform, the bishops' letter states that the present welfare system doesn't serve the poor in a way that respects their human dignity. A patchwork of programs leaves the recipients poor, allows gaps in coverage, treats the poor inconsistently, shows wide variations in benefits across the states, humiliates clients, and is loaded with bureaucratic "red tape." The public is fed misinformation, and welfare clients are stereotyped unfairly.

The letter recommends thorough reform of the welfare system and income support programs. Public assistance programs should be adequately funded so as to provide decent support. National eligibility standards and benefit levels should be established by the federal government. When left to the states or localities, it means the poor suffer far more in some places than in others. Provision should be made for annual cost-of-living adjustments and the gradual consolidation of programs, to eliminate confusion and duplication. Marriage and the family should be strengthened by the program. AFDC should be open to two-parent families, and assistance plans should not force parents to work outside the home when children need care and attention.

The bishops believe programs should encourage, not penalize, gainful employment. Welfare recipients should take part in reforming the programs, and the programs should not single out or stigmatize the poor. Administration of the programs should show respect for clients. Regulations should be no greater than for comparable programs for other citizens.

How could America go about making such reforms as

these? The bishops' letter summons the initiative and competition that are part of the national spirit—as is teamwork. Real cooperation is needed if powerful interest groups are not to veto policies essential for the common good. The bishops spell out ways that labor and management can cooperate within individual firms and industries, ways that economic growth in localities and regions can be encouraged, and ways that can build new forms of cooperation in developing national and international policies to strengthen the worldwide economy.

No such changes in our economic system will take place unless we, you and I, support and help implement them. Each individual, each citizen can contribute to improving our society. How? By taking action in our own communities and organizations. We belong to churches and synagogues, to fraternal societies, to clubs, to trade unions, to veterans' groups, to student groups, to Y's, to the Scouts. Wherever we are, if we care enough, we can help. We can suggest ways groups we belong to could influence government action against poverty. We can quite directly offer our own time and energy to ease the problems of the poor.

In Chicago the Jewish Federation launched Project Ezra to help lodge homeless Jews and meet their other needs. The members opened a shelter to provide meals, clothing, social work services, and access to job interviews. Volunteers stand by a twenty-four-hour hotline and staff the various aid projects. In New York the Riverside Church operates a Food Pantry, raising funds and distributing food—and clothing—to thousands of the hungry in their community. In East Harlem, an Interfaith

Welfare Committee, representing seven religious voluntary agencies, tracks hunger in its neighborhood and
helps to meet food emergencies.

In five southern counties of Virginia, TAP (Total Action Against Poverty) acts like a guerrilla army fighting
poverty in the Roanoke Valley. Its roster of projects runs
on and on—legal aid, food distribution, housing rehabili-
tation, on-the-job training, adult education, grass-roots
organizing, counseling for drug addicts, shelters for bat-
tered wives, and programs assisting former offenders.
TAP's story is but one of hundreds of community action
programs testifying to the human compassion of Americans. They all depend upon the decency, the imagination,
the courage of volunteers.

To carry out programs of the kind the bishops call for
will be tremendously costly. It will require considerably
higher taxes, which the bishops believe the rich, who
have given in to "excessive consumption," should pay.
The bishops say that not just the extremely wealthy but
"the richest 20 percent" would be spiritually better off if
they would cut down on personal consumption and agree
to fund more public programs which would permit "the
poor and the despised to live with dignity."

A smaller personal sacrifice would be needed if
America would spend less on arms, the bishops believe.
While military spending rose 60 percent in the first five
Reagan years, nonmilitary spending went up only 28
percent. The bishops said, "The investment of human
creativity and material resources in the production of
weapons of war . . . drains financial resources that should
be dedicated to meeting human needs."

Let's look for a moment at what the nation has actually

spent to reduce poverty. Between 1960 and 1983, overall federal spending as a share of the total national product rose 6 percentage points. Official studies show that these outlays have reduced poverty disturbingly little. The elderly and the disabled have benefited most, while single women with children and some other groups continue to suffer very high poverty rates. The number of people who are poor today remains unacceptably high, ranging from about 10 to 13 percent of the population.

Can America afford to increase the share of national income devoted to reducing poverty? Yes, if we are willing to raise the level of taxes needed to do it, as the Catholic bishops and many other groups propose. It is worth repeating that the United States spends a smaller share of national income on redistributing wealth than do most other Western industrialized nations. (West Germany spends 26.5 percent; Italy 22.7 percent; Great Britain 18.9 percent; the United States 14.9 percent, and Japan 13.8 percent—all figures as of 1981.) It is no surprise that by devoting fewer resources to reducing poverty the United States leaves a greater degree of economic inequality than that found in other countries.

Why don't we do better in helping the poor? Not for purely economic reasons. It's more for political reasons. Americans do have a strong conviction about equality when it comes to political and civil rights. But that desire for equality does not extend to economic rights. Greater economic equality would mean a greater governmental role in our society's economic arrangements. Most Americans believe the only job of government is to get out of the way and let the laws of free enterprise work. That's called the law of the market. (To the compassionate, it can look like the law of the jungle.) Those who come out poor or stay poor in the economic competition are blamed for their own weaknesses and inadequacies. The powerful who prosper in the American system find it easy to think there is nothing wrong with it. They say those who fail to prosper have themselves to blame. The rich and the poor get what each deserves.

These beliefs are so deep-rooted, it is hard to be optimistic that the condition of the American poor will soon be greatly improved. Social welfare spending rose sharply between 1960 and 1980, but in the 1980s government initiative to reduce poverty came to a stop and in many programs seems to have been reversed.

One result of this attitude toward the poor is that the government's approach to poverty is unplanned and wasteful. True, billions are spent, but the money doesn't break the cycle of poverty. Each antipoverty program aims at but one aspect of the bigger problem and ignores what all the other programs do. The approach is so fragmented, so chaotic, that it doesn't really meet the needs of the poor or get at the root cause of poverty.

The politicians know that the poor are a minority, often badly educated, weak, isolated, dispirited, disorganized. The poor command little attention from the powerful. The poor are not where the votes come from. Washington and the state capitals do not listen to the poor, do not ask what they need. In the richest nation on earth, the poor—although they can be found among all races and ages and in every region—somehow remain almost invisible.

To reduce poverty and bring about greater economic equality, Americans must take a critical look at our failures and hesitations. While poverty continues, it will do great harm to our society. Poverty, as we've seen, is a major cause of crime and delinquency. It blights our countryside, our neighborhoods, our cities. It damages America by cutting down on economic growth while increasing the cost of social programs. It cripples the physical and emotional lives of many. It keeps millions from realizing their human potential and from making their contribution to society.

That is why so many individuals and organizations are thinking hard and honestly about poverty and what to do about it. We, too, could help, if we wanted to. Can we stand by and passively accept other people's misery?

A NOTE
ON PROGRAMS
TO REDUCE POVERTY

There are three kinds of programs to reduce poverty and help equalize incomes.

The first kind distributes money or other forms of noncash aid only to poor or near-poor families. These are technically called "means-tested income transfers." It simply means that help is not provided to any but the poor and sometimes only to particular groups of the poor—the aged, the blind, the disabled, single parents and their children, and poor veterans and their families. When local, state, and federal government agencies provide this help in cash payments, it is commonly called "welfare." Most of the cash-assistance programs go back to the Social Security Act of 1935.

The noncash help is called social insurance. It has three parts—Social Security, Medicare, and unemployment insurance. These programs redistribute income from the better-off to the less well-off. The programs are largely financed by payroll taxes paid by the people currently working and their employers. Benefits are paid to groups that include retired people, the disabled, dependents of deceased workers, and people who are insured and lose their jobs.

This form of social insurance is far more popular with the public than welfare. People view it as a rightful repayment during adversity for taxes they paid during flush times. Whether people are poor, middle class, or wealthy, they are entitled to these social insurance payments.

The third type of program has aimed at reducing poverty by raising the earnings of poor people rather than by supplying aid in cash. By providing special education, training, and employment help, the program seeks to raise the future earnings of disadvantaged children and adults. The better-known methods of doing this include Project Head Start—a federal preschool program for poor children; aid targeted to certain elementary schools in poverty areas; grants for higher education; the Job Corps; and federal grants to state and local governments to plan and run employment-training programs for teenagers and adults in accordance with the special needs of their own region or community. The basic idea behind this third type of program is that by raising the quality and amount of training received by people on the bottom, they will be able to earn more, and thus the inequality of income will be reduced.

Most of these programs are referred to and defined in the text. The index will indicate where to find these references.

BIBLIOGRAPHY

After the first months of research for this book, I realized I had two aspects of poverty to cover: the personal and the general. To give the reader an idea of what it feels like to be poor in America today, I have tried to let people tell their stories in their own words as much as possible. To provide the general picture calls for the hard facts about poverty. It is impossible to avoid numbers and percentages to demonstrate increases or decreases in poverty and to compare one period of time with another and one section of the population with others. I have tried to keep such data to the minimum needed for understanding.

This is not an attempt to cover poverty completely. A book such as this can only suggest the nature of one of America's most urgent problems. I wanted this to be a short book, to be read by young and old alike, especially by those who have had no personal experience with poverty and who have no scholarly interest in the subject, but a general interest.

There is a large literature on many aspects of poverty. Check under "Poverty" and "Poor" in your library catalog and in *Books in Print*. New titles appear every year. The references below are chiefly those I used for this book. But I should call attention to other sources. The files of the *New York Times* almost daily contain news stories, feature articles, columns and Op-Ed pieces about poverty. Its coverage is of great value to the writer. Of course, as the Bibliography indicates, I read many other periodicals, too.

Another source that must be mentioned is the Institute for Research on Poverty, at the University of Wisconsin in Madison. It furnished me with more than a score of scholarly reports and analyses of poverty and policy on poverty, prepared by experts from many different institutions. I am grateful to the Institute and those who participate in its work. I am also thankful to several U.S. representatives and senators who kindly sent me federal research documents and material on their own contributions to poverty legislation. Many of these documents were prepared by the Congressional Research Service in the Library of Congress.

Students and teachers may be especially interested in the Cerny and Richardson reference below. The annotated bibliography it provides should be useful in classroom study and discussion.

Anderson, Elijah. *A Place on the Corner*. Chicago: University of Chicago Press, 1978.

Anderson, Marion. "Neither Jobs Nor Security: Women's Unemployment and the Pentagon Budget." Lansing, Mich.: Employment Research Associates, n.d.

Blumberg, Paul. *Inequality in an Age of Decline.* New York: Oxford University Press, 1980.

Cerny, Marsha, and Joe Richardson. "How Can the Federal Government Best Decrease Poverty in the United States?" A Preliminary Bibliography on the 1984–85 National High School Debate Topic. Congressional Research Service, Library of Congress, March 23, 1984.

Cobb, Edwin L. *No Ceasefires: The War on Poverty in Roanoke Valley.* Cabin John, Md.: Seven Oaks Press, 1985.

Cunningham, William. "Hunger in Detroit." *Christian Century,* April 7, 1982, pp. 423–24.

Ehrenreich, Barbara, and Frances Fox Piven. "The Feminization of Poverty." *Dissent,* Spring 1984, pp. 162–70.

Eisler, Benita. *Class Act: America's Last Dirty Secret.* New York: Franklin Watts, 1983.

Gabe, Tom. "Progress Against Poverty (1959 to 1983): The Recent Poverty Debate Updated 9/13/84." Congressional Research Service, The Library of Congress, 1984.

Galbraith, John Kenneth. *The Affluent Society.* Boston: Houghton Mifflin, 1958.

———. *The Nature of Mass Poverty.* Cambridge, Mass.: Harvard University Press, 1979.

———. *The Voice of the Poor.* Cambridge, Mass.: Harvard University Press, 1983.

Garraty, John A. *Unemployment in History.* New York: Harper and Row, 1978.

Glasgow, Douglass G. *The Black Underclass.* New York: Random House/Vintage Books, 1981.

Greenberg, Mark. "A Breakdown of Consensus," *Dissent,* Fall 1982, pp. 468–78.

Hacker, Andrew. "Welfare: The Future of an Illusion." *New York Review,* February 28, 1985, pp. 37–43.

Harrington, Michael. *The New American Poverty.* New York: Holt Rinehart Winston, 1984.

Heclo, Hugh. "The Political Foundations of Antipoverty Policy." IRP Conference Paper. Madison, Wisc.: University of Wisconsin, 1984.

Hollings, Ernest F. *The Case Against Hunger.* New York: Cowles, 1970.

Hope, Marjorie, and James Young. "The Homeless: On the Street, on the Road." *Christian Century,* January 18, 1984, pp. 48–52.

Hug, James E. "The Catholic Bishops Pick Up Another Bomb." *Christianity and Crisis,* October 1, 1984, pp. 344–48.

Kennedy, Edward M. *Going Hungry in America.* Report to the Committee on Labor and Human Resources, U.S. Senate, Dec. 22, 1983.

Komisar, Lucy. *Down and Out in the USA: A History of Public Welfare.* New York: Franklin Watts, 1977.

Kornblum, William. "Lumping the Poor." *Dissent,* Summer 1984, pp. 295–302.

Lappe, Frances Moore, and Joseph Collins. *Food First: Beyond the Myth of Scarcity.* New York: Ballantine, 1982.

Less, Walli F., and Marilyn G. Haft. *Time Without Work.* Boston: South End Press, 1983.

McElvaine, Robert S. *The Great Depression.* New York: Times Books, 1984.

Maharidge, Dale, and Michael Williamson. *Journey to Nowhere: The Saga of the New Underclass.* New York: Dial Press, 1985.

Meissner, Hanna M., ed. *Poverty in the Affluent Society.* New York: Harper and Row, 1966.

Meltzer, Milton. *Bread and Roses.* New York: Alfred Knopf, 1967.
———. *Brother Can You Spare a Dime?* New York: Alfred Knopf, 1969.
Monahan, Sharon. "Bread Line." *America,* March 14, 1981, p. 206.
National Urban League. *The State of Black America, 1985.* New York: National Urban League, 1985.
Nelson, Marcia Z. "Street People," *The Progressive,* March 1985, pp. 24–29.
Patterson, James T. *America's Struggle Against Poverty, 1900–1980.* Cambridge, Mass.: Harvard University Press, 1981.
Physicians' Task Force on Hunger in America. *Hunger in America: The Growing Epidemic.* Boston: Harvard School of Public Health, 1985.
Pinkney, Alphonso. *The Myth of Black Progress.* Cambridge, Mass.: Harvard University Press, 1984.
Piven, Frances Fox, and Richard A. Cloward. *The New Class War.* New York: Pantheon, 1982.
———. *Poor People's Movements: Why They Succeed, How They Fail.* New York: Random House/Vintage Books, 1979.
Radding, Michael. "Street People." *America,* February 18, 1984, pp. 111–12.
Reich, Robert B. "Human Capital and Economic Policy." *Dissent,* Summer 1983, pp. 307–16.
Rodgers, Harrell R., Jr. *Poverty Amid Plenty.* Reading, Mass.: Addison-Wesley, 1979.
Rubin, Lillian B. *Worlds of Pain: Life in the Working Class Family.* New York: Basic Books, 1976.
Rustin, Bayard. "Are Blacks Better Off Today?" *The Atlantic,* October 1984, pp. 121–23.
Scott, Hilda. *Working Your Way to the Bottom: The*

Feminization of Poverty. London: Pandora, 1985.

Shipp, P. Royal. "Poverty: Trends, Causes and Cures." Congressional Research Service, Library of Congress, February 1984.

"A Small Town's Last-Ditch Fight for Survival." *U.S. News & World Report,* March 11, 1985, pp. 27–28.

Thurow, Lester C. "How to Get Out of the Economic Rut." *New York Review,* February 14, 1985, pp. 9–11.

Tobier, Emanuel. *The Changing Face of Poverty.* New York: Community Service Society, 1984.

Tyler, Gus. *Scarcity: A Critique of the American Economy.* Chicago: Quadrangle, 1976.

U.S. Bishops' Pastoral Letter on Catholic Social Teaching and the U.S. Economy (First Draft). *Origins,* November 15, 1984.

U.S. Commission on Civil Rights. "A Growing Crisis: Disadvantaged Women and Their Children." May 1983.

Valentine, Charles A. *Culture and Poverty.* Chicago: University of Chicago Press, 1968.

Zinn, Howard, ed. *Justice: Eyewitness Accounts.* Boston: Beacon Press, 1974.

INDEX